One Boy's Destiny
Two Men Prepare

Series: Forever His Destiny Series

Book: 3

By

Nathan Leigh Moffett

Table of Contents

Acknowledgement

I must offer my thanks to the Almighty God of the Bible, YAHWEH, who guided this entire journey. He provided the dreams, the visions, and the daily insights that shaped every page. This book is a testimony to His faithfulness—I am merely the pen in His hand.

(1) The Last First Day

Disney's Enchantment Realm shimmered beneath the morning sun—an entire kingdom of imagination made real. Crystal spires, floating lanterns, pathways that glowed under children's footsteps. Entire rides powered not just by engineering but by whatever cosmic wonder Nathan had quietly poured into them during the last three years.

And today… He stepped down.

Nathan stood at the balcony of the Realm Director's tower, overlooking the park that had become his love letter to the world. Gabriel stood beside him, arm around his waist, Tyler leaning comfortably into Nathan's other side.

"Looks like a dream," Tyler whispered.

"It *was* a dream," Nathan murmured. "And now it belongs to the world."

Later that morning, before the gates opened, Nathan signed the final document relinquishing his title. It wasn't sadness that crossed his face… it was peace. He pressed the pen down gently, as if blessing the paper.

"From this day," the board chair announced warmly, "Nathan Leigh Moffett becomes Ambassador-at-Large for the Enchantment Realm. He may appear at any ride, event, celebration… entirely at his own choosing."

Nathan winked. "Translation: I get free rides forever."

Tyler whooped. Gabriel laughed. Cameras flashed. Magic—both manmade and otherworldly—seemed to hum in the air.

But underneath all that celebration… something else hummed too.

A shift. Power gathering. Something Nathan wasn't talking about yet.

That evening, in their private suite overlooking the fireworks, Tyler sat cross-legged on the carpet, unusually quiet. Nathan and Gabriel exchanged a look—this was not a child who stayed quiet for long unless something was clawing at him inside.

"Dad? Papa?" Tyler asked, voice small for the first time in months. "Can we talk? Just… the three of us?"

Nathan lowered immediately onto the floor with him. Gabriel followed.

Tyler swallowed. "I'm scared. You both keep getting more powerful. Papa, your hands glowed yesterday. Dad, you… You lifted a whole hover-platform like it weighed nothing. And lately, I keep seeing things. Past things. Future things. I don't know what's happening, and I don't want to lose either of you as a result of everything that's happening."

Nathan's heart split just a little.

Gabriel's breath caught.

Nathan cupped Tyler's face gently. "Hey… look at me. You don't lose what is eternal, sweetheart. But you're right. Things *are* changing."

Tyler blinked. "Are you getting sick?"

"No," Nathan said softly. But he didn't look away.

Tyler's brows pinched together. "Then why does it feel like… like you're walking somewhere I can't follow?"

Gabriel's hand tightened around Nathan's knee.

Nathan exhaled slowly. Time for truth.

"There are people chosen for long earthly lives," he said. "And others appointed for shorter ones with far greater purpose. I don't know which I am. I only know this: whatever time I have, I will spend it helping you both become everything God intended."

Gabriel froze. "Nathan…"

Tyler's eyes filled with tears. "So you *are* leaving?"

Nathan pulled him fully into his arms. Tyler clung like he was a toddler again. "No. I'm here. I'm staying. But one day—far ahead or closer than we want—there will be a moment when I'm called away. And I want you ready, Tyler. I want you strong. Wise. Capable. Leading people, not chasing powers."

Tyler whispered into his shoulder, "But I want to be strong like you."

Nathan smiled faintly. "Batman never had powers. But his discernment, his courage, his unshakable ideals? Those changed the world."

Gabriel added softly, "Some abilities… they're a burden. Let us carry them."

Tyler sniffed but nodded slowly.

Nathan kissed his forehead. "But… if you truly seek greatness, then there *is* a path. Not powers. Not cosmic fire. But something older. Ancestral. A leadership gauntlet that shapes the heart more than the body. If you choose to face it… It may forge you into the man you dream of becoming."

Tyler wiped his face. "I want to try."

Nathan brushed his hair back. "Then we will guide you."

Night settled. Tyler slept.

Gabriel sat beside Nathan on the balcony, fireworks painting them in shifting color. "Why didn't you tell me sooner?" he asked gently, staring at the skyline instead of his husband. "That you might… leave before your time?"

Nathan leaned into him. "Because saying it out loud makes it real."

Gabriel shut his eyes. Pain flickered through him—raw, quiet, private.

Nathan rested his head against Gabriel's shoulder. "I'll be with you for a long time, Gabriel. Long enough to rebuild the estate. Long enough to find every lost branch of your family. Long enough to see Tyler become a leader. But there will come a day when my path diverges from yours, and no man will know when."

Gabriel swallowed hard. "And I'm supposed to accept that?"

"No," Nathan whispered. "You're supposed to live fiercely until then."

Gabriel turned his face into Nathan's hair and breathed him in. "I'm not losing you."

"Not today," Nathan said softly. "Not soon. Maybe not for decades. But we must raise Tyler knowing the world will one day need him."

―――――――――――――――――――

The estate had become a beacon—light shimmering from the cavern beneath it, ancient wards reawakening after centuries asleep.

And before Gabriel had even begun searching for the lost lineage…

―――――――――――――――――――

Families. Strangers. Faces that looked startlingly similar to Gabriel's childhood photos. People holding old maps, journals, and crests that matched the sigils etched into the cavern walls.

The first ancestor knelt before Nathan and Gabriel and said:

"We felt the call of home."

Behind them, the land was already transforming—surveyors marking out mega village districts, architects sketching defense rings, agricultural paddocks beginning to bloom with life from soil that hadn't seen growth in generations.

The world was shifting.

Their son was awakening.

And somewhere deep inside himself…Nathan felt the first trembling hint of the day he had not yet named.

(2) The Council Forms

By morning, the estate felt different.

Not louder—though new voices drifted through the halls— not fuller—though dozens of families set up temporary lodging tents across the farmland— but *older,* as if the land itself remembered it was never meant to sleep this long.

Nathan woke first. He was partially levitating above the bed and as he began to come back to reality, he wafted back on the bed just as he swung his feet to the floor.

Gabriel still breathed softly on his side. During the night, an arm draped over Nathan's waist, grounding him in the comfort of a man who always dreamed like he was protecting something. By morning's first light, he huddled away from Nathan because of the levitation. Tyler had curled up in an armchair across the room sometime during the night, a blanket half-slid off his shoulder. He had come in and was worried about something yet afraid to disturb his dads.

For one suspended moment, Nathan stared at them both, looking back and forth and reveling in their similar expressions and uncanny movements.

The world had shifted yesterday. It would shift again today. Would they be ready for it?

He walked quietly, almost resuming his levitation walk, kissed Tyler's temple on the way to the door, and stepped out into the morning light.

A temporary pavilion had been raised near the cavern entrance— simple beams, open sides, long tables made of boards laid over crates. Ancestral families moved with purpose, arranging boxes, scrolls, and artifacts. The smell of earth and old leather drifted through the air.

Gabriel arrived moments later, Tyler rubbing sleep from his eyes as he walked beside him.

When Gabriel stepped under the pavilion, the talking softened and the people parted in reverence to his presence.

Somehow these people recognized him—not his face, but something deeper. Lineage. Calling. Blood memory. An elder woman stepped forward and placed a weathered book in Gabriel's hands.

"This is yours," she said. "Your family carried it since before captivity."

Tyler leaned in with excitement. Nathan held himself back, staying a step behind—not claiming space that wasn't his, not intruding on a heritage he had only been grafted into by love.

More boxes opened.

Items were laid out for examination:

- stone tablets etched with spiraling sigils
- scrolls sealed with wax of a symbol matching the cavern walls
- journals describing migrations across deserts and seas
- a faded sketch of a person enslaved beside another enslaved person

The council settled into a half-circle.

Right now it was small— **Gabriel as heir, Tyler as vision-bearer in training, and Nathan as the man who stood outside the circle but safeguarded the council.**

Gabriel began reading from the journal placed before him.

"Our people were taken into captivity," Gabriel read quietly, his voice carrying through the pavilion, "but not alone. They describe laboring beside the Hebrews. Praying with them. Waiting for deliverance with them."

An elder nodded. "We were in Egypt, Gabriel. Not merely *near* Israel—*with* Israel. Under the same chains."

Something inside Nathan tensed—so sharply, so involuntarily—that several ancestors nearest him turned their heads. Before anyone could speak, a sudden rush of wind erupted around him, bending grass and stirring dust in a spiraling column.

And Nathan was gone.

Not teleported—*escorted*. Lifted and carried by something unseen, something divine, something that recognized him.

In a blink, he had been moved nearly a hundred meters into the open field, facing the distant direction where Egypt would lie on any map. The movement took mere milliseconds, but to Nathan it felt like being drawn through honeyed time—slow, stretched, meaningful.

His hands rose on their own.

His tunic fluttered around his arms.

His palms extended toward the horizon— the exact posture of a man he had only ever read about.

A man named Moses.

Back beneath the pavilion, Gabriel felt the wind whip past and instinctively turned—his body alert, his heart dropping.

But he continued reading, voice unsteady and yet still occasionally looking toward where Nathan had been taken:

"'When the plagues struck, we sheltered with them. And when the waters parted, we crossed with them. When Moses raised his staff, we saw the sea stand like walls of glass.'"

Nathan's breath trembled out of him. He could hear the passage being read as if he were next to Gabriel.

His hands shook.

The world tilted—and suddenly his sandals pressed into *desert sand.*

In Korinthos, morning light warmed the fields. But in the vision— the ancient event— Night was falling.

A cold wind slammed into his chest with the weight of memory older than any mortal lifetime. It tore at his tunic, carried the scent of brine and fear and faith.

Before him:

- The angel of the Lord and the pillar of cloud shift position, shielding the Hebrews' backs.
- The Red Sea dividing, walls of water gleaming with light from the cloud pillar behind them.
- Thunder cracking like heaven's heartbeat.
- Hebrew families running between shimmering towers of water that reflected the pillar's glow.
- Moses, arms raised, silhouette ablaze with divine authority.

Nathan felt splashes of water across his face—*real* water—cold, salty, stinging. His hands remained raised as he walked with them across the dry seabed.

Back in the pavilion, droplets materialized in the air and landed on the back of Gabriel's neck. He jerked, startled, then felt the unmistakable pull—*Nathan.* He swung onto a nearby horse in a single motion, Tyler scrambling up behind him as they galloped toward the field.

In the vision, Nathan gasped as his feet left the ground— he rose, weightless— and accelerated across the seabed at impossible speed. He was placed atop a tall rock overlooking the passage.

He watched the final group of people climb to safety.

The pillar of cloud dissipated.

And the Egyptian chariots thundered into the dry corridor— horses screaming, soldiers frenzied, driven mad by a force beyond reason.

As the last chariot entered the great divide, the walls of water collapsed.

The sea roared shut.

Silence swallowed the valley.

Another scene burst into being—

Nathan now stood upon a mountain ridge, watching Moses from afar as though in a cinematic vision.

Moses cradled two stone tablets glowing faintly with divine etching.

God's presence burned across the sky like living flame.

Moses descended, saw the golden calf, and— in agony— shattered the tablets.

The scene shifted again:

Now Moses climbed the mountain once more, alone. He carved new tablets himself— Every chisel strike a prayer, Every breath is a surrender.

Nathan felt the mountain's heat.

The loneliness of leadership.

The crushing ache of a man called to lead his people to the border of promise but never cross with them.

And Nathan *knew.*

He knew the echo. He knew the warning.

I will help them gather Gabriel's lineage. I will help raise Tyler to stand where no other can. But I... may not step foot into their completed world.

The vision shattered like glass.

Nathan's presence snapped back into the echo of reality— this time atop the high ridge overlooking the tribal lands.

His knees wobbled. He stumbled, catching himself on a tree trunk, chest heaving.

Below, Gabriel arrived on horseback, Tyler clinging to him. Gabriel slid off and cupped his hands around his mouth.

"Nathan—what did you see?"

Nathan forced air into his lungs. He bent over, hands on his knees, trembling.

"Not now. Not yet!" he shouted, voice cracking.

Tyler stared up at him, wide-eyed, terrified. Even from that distance, Nathan felt the boy's fear hit him like a physical blow.

He turned away, unable to hold Tyler's gaze.

Not yet. Not this fear. Not for him.

When the council adjourned for the midday meal, Nathan slipped away to the storage house, needing a moment to himself.

He pressed both hands to the cool stone wall.

Why Moses? Why that? Why now? Are you telling me… I won't see the finished promise, like I'll die or be left behind?

No voice answered.

But the silence felt like confirmation.

Nathan wiped his face, forced composure, and set himself to work gathering gear—packs, map satchels, tools. The expeditions would begin soon. Gabriel would lead them.

Tyler would grow into whatever God was shaping him to become.

Nathan? He would prepare the way. And pray he had more time than the mountain suggested.

Nathan was tightening the straps on a supply pack when he heard a sound—a sharp inhale, a gasp, and then a thud.

"Nathan!"

Gabriel's voice, frantic.

Nathan sprinted.

He found Gabriel crouched beside Tyler. The boy stood rigid, eyes glazed with a light not of this world. Gold flecks shimmered around his pupils like tiny pieces of dawn.

Tyler lifted his hand, fingers trembling, and light flickered between them—soft, hesitant, searching.

When he spoke, it wasn't fully his voice:

"The blood remembers. The land awakens. And the heir begins to see."

Tyler's knees buckled.

Nathan caught him before he hit the ground a second time.

"Papa… Dad…" Tyler whispered weakly as consciousness returned. "I saw… something."

Nathan gathered him close. "It's alright. You're safe. Tell us what you saw."

Tyler shook his head, breath trembling.

"It wasn't the past this time," he whispered. "It was the *future.* And I think… I think we're not ready."

Nathan and Gabriel exchanged a look.

And for the first time since the caverns… Nathan truly didn't know what was coming.

(3) The Vision of the Heir

Tyler had barely regained consciousness when Nathan carried him back inside. His body felt lighter than normal in Nathan's arms—almost shimmering. Gabriel walked beside them, steadying Nathan when the aftershock of his own experience made his knees wobble.

They laid Tyler gently on a cushioned bench in the council hall. Nathan knelt beside him, brushing sweat-soaked hair from the boy's forehead.

"Tyler," he whispered. "Sweetheart. You're safe. Breathe with me."

Slowly, Tyler opened his eyes.

Not the bright, mischievous eyes Nathan adored— but eyes rimmed with gold, the last residue of whatever force had spoken through him.

"Dad?" Tyler breathed. "Papa?"

Gabriel took his hand. Nathan took the other.

"We're right here," Gabriel said.

Tyler swallowed hard. "I… I saw something. Two somethings. Past and future. They were tangled together."

Nathan nodded gently. "Tell us only what you can."

Tyler took a shaky breath and closed his eyes as if the vision still hovered behind his eyelids.

"I saw… the land full of people. Our people." His fingers tightened around Gabriel's. "They were returning from everywhere. Like the ground itself was calling them home."

Nathan exchanged a glance with Gabriel. The timing. The accuracy. Exactly as the ancestors had described the ancient return after Egypt… and exactly what was happening now.

"But then," Tyler whispered, "the vision jumped."

He sat up slowly, voice trembling.

"I saw a day when the whole tribe is finally together. When our lands are rebuilt. When everything is ready. When the world is waiting for you both to lead everyone into the new age."

He looked between them…

…and then hesitated.

Gabriel leaned in. "Tyler? What frightened you?"

Tyler's voice cracked.

"In the vision… You both were there. Papa, you were wearing that crest of leadership they keep talking about. Dad, you were shining so bright the sky reflected you." His breath caught. "But then—then the light flickered. And you—Dad—"

Nathan's heart stopped.

Tyler's voice was nearly a whisper:

"You weren't there anymore."

Silence crushed the room.

Nathan forced calm into his voice. "Did you see harm? Pain? Anything like that?"

Tyler shook his head fiercely. "No. Not death. Just… absence. A sudden absence. Like something pulled you out of the picture. Like you were called somewhere I couldn't follow."

Tears spilled over Tyler's cheeks. "Dad, I don't want to lose you. Not ever. Not even a little."

Nathan pulled him into a tight embrace, holding him until the shaking eased.

"I'm here," he murmured into Tyler's hair. "And visions don't define destiny. They show possibilities, not certainties."

Gabriel sat beside them, running a hand through Tyler's curls, heart aching at the sight of both of them clinging to each other.

But the look Gabriel gave Nathan above Tyler's head said everything:

This is exactly what Nathan feared. And Tyler had seen it too.

Tyler had finally drifted to sleep in his room, exhausted by prophecy and panic. Nathan tucked the blankets around him, kissed his forehead, and stood watching him for a long time.

Gabriel waited in the hallway, arms crossed tightly—not in anger, but bracing for truth.

"Walk with me," Nathan whispered.

They slipped out the back exit, past the construction scaffolds, past the lantern-lit pathways, into the quiet grove overlooking the ridge where Nathan had stood earlier.

When they were alone, Gabriel grabbed Nathan's arm gently but firmly.

"Tell me what happened," he said. "All of it. No more holding anything back."

Nathan's shoulders sagged under a weight too heavy for any one man. He looked up at the ridge.

And the words came.

"I didn't just see the Exodus. I *was* there. Or something like it. I felt Moses' footsteps in my feet. I felt the tablets in my arms. I felt the judgment, the heartbreak, the calling."

Gabriel waited, jaw tight, eyes burning.

"And then," Nathan said, voice faltering, "I saw the moment Moses knew he wouldn't enter the Promised Land."

A crack ran through Gabriel's composure.

Nathan looked down at his hands. "And I knew. Not because of fear. Because God told me the truth without speaking, I will help gather your lineage. I will help prepare the land. I will help raise Tyler into the man he must be. But the final completion?" His breath trembled. "I won't be here for it."

Gabriel shook his head. "No. No, Nathan. That can't—"

"Gabe…"

Gabriel's chest rose sharply. His eyes shone with wet fury and grief. "You're my husband. My heart. My partner. You do not get to disappear into some divine calling without me. I don't accept it."

Nathan cupped Gabriel's face, thumbs brushing his cheeks.

"This isn't about acceptance. It's about preparation."

Gabriel turned his face away, voice breaking. "I can't lose you."

Nathan pressed his forehead to Gabriel's. "You won't. Not for a long time. But one day—"

"No." Gabriel's voice cracked into a whisper.

Nathan kissed him gently. "One day, the world will need you and Tyler more than it needs me."

Gabriel closed his eyes, breathing hard.

Neither man noticed the quiet footsteps behind the grove.

Tyler hadn't meant to follow them.

(4) The Awakening and Follow

(Tyler's POV)

I awoke suddenly—heart pounding, breath sharp, as if someone had whispered my name from far away. Not a voice, not a dream… a pull. A tug deep in my chest that said:

Go outside. Find them.

So, I slipped out of bed, careful not to wake the house, and crept barefoot through the hall. The night air was cold against my skin as I reached the back door. In the distance, I saw two silhouettes walking toward the grove—Nathan's soft, familiar gait and Gabriel's steady, protective stride.

I decided to follow. Quiet. Hidden.

My curiosity only lead me closer and made me want to hear what was being said. Maybe I might feel safe again after the vision if I knew more of what was really happening. I needed to know my parents were truly okay.

I didn't expect to hear anything. I didn't expect my world to break.

My timing placed me behind a tree just as Nathan said:

"I won't be there to see the completion."

My body froze in place, and my face crinkled in horror.

What?

Nathan's voice came again—gentler, heartbreaking.

"I'll help gather your lineage. I'll help raise Tyler to stand where no one else can. But the final promise… I won't be here for it."

Something inside me cracked like thin ice.

No. No, that can't be right. I just saw him shining brighter than anyone. I saw him leading us. I saw him alive.

Gabriel's voice shook. Dad was so broken. Never ever had I heard him like that—angry and hurting at the same time.

"You're my husband. My everything. You don't get to disappear into some divine calling without me."

My stomach twisted.

Disappear? Divine calling? Nathan… leaving?

The air around me thinned. I found I couldn't breathe well.

Nathan spoke again, softer—too soft.

"One day, the world will need you and Tyler more than it needs me."

And that's when I completely broke. Because suddenly the vision made sense.

The moment Nathan disappeared. The empty space where his light had been. The sudden absence that wasn't death… but something worse.

He was telling the truth. He really won't be here. Not at the end. Not when everything is done. Not when we finally find everyone. Not when we're safe. Not when our tribe stands together. Not when Dad leads. Not when I…

My chest constricted again causing me to clutch my body in desperation.

Not when I become whatever I'm supposed to become.

Tears blurred everything. I pressed a hand over my mouth to keep from making a sound.

Then, my thoughts spiraled out of control.

Why didn't he tell me? Why didn't they think I could handle it? How am I supposed to lead anything if the person who made me brave won't be there? Why give me visions if all they do is show me the worst thing I could ever imagine? How do I keep going when the future starts with losing Nathan? What kind of destiny takes away the person who loves me the most? I don't want this role. I don't want powers. I don't want visions. I just want my dads. Both of them. Together. Forever.

Every promise they ever gave me— that we would be a family, that we would face everything together, that nothing on Earth or heaven could tear us apart—

It all felt like it had shattered to pieces at my feet.

Why would God choose this? Why choose me? Why choose Nathan for something that pulls him away? Why make me watch this future happen?

Tears dripped onto my bare feet, and the Earth beneath me blurred.

Gabriel whispered brokenly, "I can't lose you."

Nathan murmured back, "You won't. Not for a long time."

But "a long time" suddenly felt like a countdown.

And this, I couldn't bear any of it.

Quietly, I stepped back—silent, trembling—into the shadows. Then another step. And another.

At first, I didn't run.

Running would make noise. Running would make them find me. Running would mean facing them.

At this time, in this moment, I couldn't do that.

Not with this truth crushing my lungs like a vice.

So, I turned away— heart ripping in two— and let the darkness swallow me as I disappeared into the grove.

For the first time in my life…

I didn't want the future he'd been shown. I didn't want the destiny everyone assumed would fit my life. I didn't want to be the heir.

All I wanted in this life were my dads. Both of them. Together. Unbroken. Safe.

It was difficult to know if the world would ever give me that again.

(5) The Vanishing Thread

Nathan's POV

The night had been almost unnaturally calm. A deceptive hush hung over the grove, the kind that makes the soul restless, like the moment before thunder when the air itself holds its breath. Gabriel and I walked back slowly, shoulders brushing in the familiar, grounding rhythm we'd perfected over months of carrying impossible things together—prophecy, miracles, fatherhood. My hand had just grazed the small of his back when it hit.

A wrongness. Not pain. Not sound. A shiver that crawled beneath my skin like ice water poured directly into my veins. The world didn't crack; it tilted—half a degree, maybe less—but enough that every atom in my body screamed *misaligned*. My breath snagged, sharp and shallow. The oxygen tasted metallic, wrong, as though someone had replaced the night air with something forged in panic.

I stopped dead.

Gabriel felt the shift in me the way he always did—like a sixth sense tuned only to my heartbeat. He turned instantly, eyes narrowing, voice already edged with the quiet, lethal fear that belonged only to parents. "Nathan?"

I couldn't answer. My pupils contracted to pinpoints, the world sharpening to painful, crystalline edges. The golden thread—the living, breathing cord that had tethered me to Tyler since the night we claimed him, since the healing, since the first time he called me "Papa" in a sleepy mumble—that thread didn't fray. It snapped. Clean. Violent. Like a guitar string severed under maximum tension, the recoil whipped through my soul.

Gone. Just… gone.

My heart stuttered—once, twice—like it had forgotten how to beat without that counter-rhythm. "He's gone," I breathed. The words tasted like ash and copper.

Gabriel blinked hard, confusion warring with the rising tide of terror. "What do you mean by 'gone'? He's asleep. We tucked him in twenty minutes ago—kissed his forehead, turned off the lamp—"

"No." My voice cracked, raw and ragged. "I can't feel him. The bond—something's severed it completely." My jaw locked so tight my teeth ached. "Something's wrong. Terribly, catastrophically wrong."

Memories flashed unbidden: Tyler's small hand in mine during the spring miracle. His laughter when I lifted him into the sky for the first time. The way his breathing evened when I whispered prayers over him at night. All of it—silenced.

In the space between one heartbeat and the next, the world narrowed to a single imperative.

No questions. No hesitation. Only the nuclear, primal surge of parental terror igniting every nerve, every muscle, every scrap of power I possessed.

I launched first—light exploding from the soles of my feet in a brilliant corona, air spiraling into violent, glowing curls as I rocketed upward. The night tore around me. Gabriel followed half a heartbeat later, ripping ragged wind currents behind him like torn fabric. We streaked across the estate like twin falling stars, fear and love fused into something unstoppable, something holy and savage.

We landed so hard the flagstone courtyard cracked beneath our boots—fissures spiderwebbing outward in sharp, accusing lines.

"Tyler!" Gabriel's roar thundered down the hallway, voice raw with a desperation I had never heard in him before—not even in battle, not even facing the Bridge.

I was right behind him, heart slamming against my ribs so violently I thought it might crack my sternum.

The bedroom door slammed open with enough force to splinter the frame and send the brass knob skittering across the floor.

Bed—empty. Sheets—thrown aside in frantic haste, still holding the faint ghost of his body heat. Window—ajar, curtains billowing inward like frightened white ghosts caught in a draft. A single sneaker lay abandoned on the rug, laces untied, as though he'd kicked it off in mid-flight.

Gabriel swore—a low, guttural sound torn from somewhere primal—and tore through the room: closet doors ripped open, hangers clattering; bathroom light snapped on, mirror reflecting only our frantic faces; dresser drawers yanked out, spilling clothes and childhood treasures across the floor as if Tyler could have somehow folded himself into a drawer and disappeared.

I moved more slowly. Not because the panic was less—God, no, it was eating me alive—but because I was listening. Reaching. Desperately groping for that faint, golden spiritual thread that had always hummed between us, steady as a heartbeat.

Nothing. No warmth. No echo. Just a vast, hollow silence that clawed at the inside of my chest, cold and absolute.

I pressed a hand to my sternum as though I could physically force the bond back into existence. My throat burned. "He's out of range… or something's blocking him. Deliberately."

Gabriel spun, face pale and furious, eyes wild with guilt and terror. "Why would he block you? Why would he do that? He's thirteen, Nathan—he doesn't even know how—"

The truth rose like bile. I hated saying it. Hated that it was even possible.

"He heard us," I whispered, voice fracturing. "He heard what I said in the grove. About destiny. About the road ahead. About… leaving."

Gabriel's face crumpled—actually crumpled—like someone had reached inside his chest and squeezed the life from his heart. His knees buckled for half a second before he caught himself against the bedpost. "Oh God… Tyler, no… my boy…"

I grabbed his hand, fingers locking tight, bruising. "Gabriel. We find him. Now."

We burst through the doors and shot skyward again—two blazing streaks of light tearing across the night sky, fear and love and guilt fused into something unstoppable.

Somewhere below, in the dark, our son was running. Barefoot. Heartbroken. Convinced the future wanted to take him away from us.

And we would tear the world apart to bring him home.

(6) The Fall and the Vision

Tyler's POV

The night wind sliced against my bare skin like knives as I ran—feet numb on cold stone, breath coming in ragged gasps that burned my lungs. I didn't have a destination. I only had direction: away.

Away from the grove. Away from the truth. Away from the future I couldn't bear to carry.

The cavern entrance loomed ahead—a black, yawning mouth in the hillside, pulsing faintly with the old, ancient power the elders whispered about. I stumbled toward it, arms wrapped tight around myself, trying to hold in the pieces that felt like they were flying apart.

I'd overheard the returning ancestors in hushed tones: "The caverns distort spiritual senses." "They block the sight." "They hide what doesn't want to be found."

Perfect.

I slipped inside.

The air turned damp and thick, heavy with the smell of wet mineral and centuries of stillness. Echoes crawled along the stone walls—faint hums of power that prickled my skin like static. But the deeper I went, the quieter everything became. The world above swallowed whole. The golden thread that had always tugged gently between me and my father was gone. Muffled. Silent.

I found a narrow exit tunnel that spat me out onto a remote ridge beyond the tribal boundaries—wild, uncharted land where even the stars seemed colder, more distant.

My breath fogged in sharp white bursts. My heart hammered so hard I tasted blood.

I could almost hear them—Papa Nathan's voice calling my name, Dad's roar of fear—but the cavern's shielding wrapped around me like a thick, muffling blanket.

Good, I thought bitterly, tears stinging. They shouldn't find me yet. Not until I—

The thought shattered at a low, guttural growl.

I spun.

A massive catlike creature prowled toward me—fur bristling like steel needles, eyes glowing pale, sickly green, body rippling with coiled muscle.

I stumbled backward. All the fear I'd been choking down surged up at once, hot and choking.

"No—stop—please—!"

It lunged.

I twisted— My foot slipped on loose scree, causing me to fall with a sharp thud and twinge.

My scream ripped through the night as I plummeted down the jagged slope—smashing against rock, tearing through brush, pain exploding in white-hot bursts until a jutting stone shelf caught me with brutal violence.

My leg bent at a sickening angle. My arm cracked beneath me like dry wood. Pain detonated through every nerve, so intense the world grayed at the edges.

The creature snarled above, pacing the ridge, hunting, waiting.

I whimpered, trying to drag myself backward, but my body refused. Everything hurt. Everything spun.

And then—

The vision hit.

It didn't feel holy. It didn't feel guided. It felt like panic weaponized.

Reality tore open like wet paper.

I saw Papa Nathan swallowed into darkness—gone. I saw Dad vanishing into blinding light—gone. I saw the tribe burning, homes shattered, smoke rising like funeral pyres. I saw myself standing alone in the wreckage—crying, screaming, powerless.

The ground crumbled beneath my feet. The sky cracked like glass. I heard my own voice echoing from somewhere deep inside, raw and desperate:

"I CAN'T DO THIS! I DON'T WANT THIS! STOP—STOP—STOP—"

The vision obeyed.

It shattered into blackness.

I collapsed, panting, half-conscious on the cold stone shelf, blood pooling beneath me.

And I cried. Broken. Bleeding. Alone.

Footsteps echoed faintly from the shadows above.

A boy appeared—fourteen, maybe fifteen—carrying a small pack and a lantern staff. His eyes widened in horror.

"Tyler Michaels?!"

I tried to lift my head. Only managed a whimper.

He scrambled down the slope, slipping, scraping knees raw, desperate.

"Oh—oh no, you're hurt. You're really hurt." His voice shook violently. "Don't move. Please don't move."

He jammed the base of his lantern staff into the ground.

A brilliant red beam shot upward—straight into the sky, cutting the darkness like fire.

Then another outpost answered. And another. And another.

Within seconds, the entire tribal network blazed in cascading red warnings.

The boy knelt beside me, trembling so hard his teeth chattered. "They're coming. Your fathers—they're gonna fly here, right?" He pressed shaking hands to my shoulders. "Don't die, okay? I'm not letting you die."

My eyes fluttered. "I'm… trying…"

The creature roared above.

The boy screamed and threw himself over me protectively.

Gabriel and Nathan hit the ridge like twin meteors.

Gabriel landed first—sliding down the slope in a blaze of power, roar shaking loose stones from the cliff. The beast snarled and retreated into darkness.

Nathan arrived half a breath later—glowing, furious, terrified— dropping to my side, scooping me into his arms with trembling gentleness.

"My baby—my baby—Tyler, look at me," he whispered, voice cracking like thin ice. "I've got you. You're safe. Just breathe, sweetheart."

Tears streaked my dirt-stained cheeks. "Papa Nathan… Dad… I'm sorry…"

Gabriel reached us, dropping to his knees, pressing his forehead to my uninjured hand, shaking. "No. No apologies. Ever. You hear me? You're our son. We come for you. Always."

Nathan nodded, tears slipping down his face. "Always."

They held me between them—one on each side—as if trying to stitch our family back together with their arms alone.

The young ancestor boy stood back, trembling with adrenaline, eyes wide.

Nathan gave him a deep, reverent nod—silent gratitude.

Gabriel lifted me gently into his arms, wings of force flaring behind him. Nathan lifted the boy to safety.

Then the three of us flew home—holding me close the entire way.

Later, in my room, soft lamps glowed. Bandages wrapped my limbs. Nathan stroked my hair. Gabriel sat on the other side, arms crossed but shaking.

The air shifted.

A warm breeze passed through the sealed room.

Light blossomed.

A figure stepped into existence—tall, radiant, armored in silver and dawn.

The archangel Gabriel.

His presence hummed like heaven's own chord.

Nathan bowed his head. Gabriel dropped to one knee.

I blinked awake at the glow.

The archangel smiled softly. "Hello, child."

I swallowed. "Are you… My Dad?"

He chuckled gently. "No. But he is named after me. And I am honored to share that name—and a slight resemblance."

Tears filled my eyes. "Everything's wrong. I saw Papa disappear. I saw Dad leaving. I saw the world break. I don't want it. I don't want any of it."

He sat beside me, brushing a luminous hand through my hair. The touch felt like peace. Like warmth. Like home.

"Visions born from fear distort the truth," he said softly. "They take the shape of your deepest wound, not your destiny."

"Am I going to lose them?"

"No," he whispered. "Not the way you fear. Love is not taken. Nor abandoned. Nor stolen by prophecy."

"Then… what did I see?"

His eyes—compassion older than stars—softened. "A glimpse of a future you are not yet ready to carry. A future still fluid… still forming… a future you will never—never—walk alone."

Tears slowed. Eyelids fluttered shut as truth settled like a blanket.

He bent and pressed a kiss to my brow—sunrise in human form. "Rest now, young heir. You are held. You are guided. And you are deeply, endlessly loved."

Sleep pulled me under—soft, peaceful, dreamless.

The angel straightened, turned to Nathan, and whispered words meant only for him:

"The Almighty has placed healing within you. Use it freely upon anyone who suffers. Call upon His name, and both flesh and spirit will answer. For by the evidence of His power working through you… They will see God in you."

Nathan's breath caught, awe and holy fear flickering across his face.

The archangel stepped back—light gathering, unfolding like wings of dawn.

He bowed once, in reverence to the mission ahead.

And dissolved into radiant brilliance.

The room dimmed to candlelight.

Nathan wiped a tear, overcome. Gabriel exhaled a long, trembling breath. And I—precious, wounded, chosen—slept without fear at last.

(7) Healing in the Morning Light

Tyler woke to warmth.

It wasn't the electric, blinding warmth of a vision or a miracle—but the soft, steady warmth of safety. The morning sun filtered through the curtains, laying gentle golden bars across his blankets. His body ached, deep and throbbing, but the pain was muted… softened by medication and sleep.

He blinked slowly, realizing he wasn't alone.

Gabriel was asleep in the chair beside him, arms folded across his chest, head tilted forward in a posture that spoke of exhaustion defeating vigilance. His legs were still braced as if he were ready to leap up at the slightest sound.

Nathan was asleep too—half-slumped over the side of the bed, his hand resting protectively where Tyler's broken leg had been. Even unconscious, Nathan's fingers curled as though still guarding him.

For a moment, Tyler simply lay there, staring at them, letting his heart expand inside his chest until it almost hurt.

I'm not alone, he remembered. *I won't be alone.*

The angel's words had wrapped themselves around his fears during the night, quieting them like a lullaby sung from heaven's gates.

He exhaled, tension melting from his shoulders.

A soft knock broke the silence.

A nurse entered quietly—a calm, middle-aged woman dressed in soft tan scrubs embroidered with the emblem of the tribal hospice. Gabriel had insisted on the best care possible. "Spare no expense," he had barked hours earlier. "Treat him like royalty."

And, by the look of the equipment arranged around the room, the staff had taken him at his word.

"Good morning, sweetheart," the nurse whispered as she stepped softly into the dim room. "I didn't mean to wake anyone."

But Nathan stirred instantly.

His eyelids flew open— and for a split second, a fiery burst of protective light flared across the room, instinctive and fierce, illuminating every corner as if he were ready to defend his family from an unseen threat.

Gabriel jerked awake an instant later, posture snapping upright so fast his spine audibly cracked. His arm shot out in front of Tyler before he even registered the nurse's presence, shielding his son on pure reflex.

"Oh my!" the nurse gasped, stumbling back a step. Her hand flew to her chest. "I—I'm only here for Tyler's vitals!"

The glow faded from Nathan's eyes as his breath steadied. He lifted a hand in apology, the tension melting from his shoulders as quickly as it had come.

The nurse gave an awkward, trembling laugh before collecting herself. She stepped closer with a kind smile. "Quite a protective father duo," she said to Tyler.

"You have no idea." Tyler quipped.

"Right. Um, then the surgeon will come assess your injuries for the scheduled surgery."

Tyler's stomach dropped.

Surgery.

The word hit him like a stone. He knew it was logical. He knew it made sense. But dread crept up his throat all the same—cold, heavy, unwelcome.

He swallowed hard, fingers curling into the blanket as both his fathers leaned protectively toward him.

Nathan caught it—of course he did. His hand slid gently over Tyler's.

"It's okay," Nathan murmured, voice soft as a warm blanket. "Just let them look."

The nurse took Tyler's temperature, pulse, and blood oxygen. She hummed approval, scribbled notes, and stepped aside as the tribal surgeon entered—a tall, lean man with intense eyes and steady hands.

He inspected the monitors, then approached Tyler with practiced calm. "Let's see how bad the swelling is today."

Nathan and Gabriel shifted instinctively closer, forming a protective arc around their son.

Then Nathan leaned in, his lips brushing Gabriel's ear. His whisper was barely a breath.

"Gabriel… God granted me the ability to heal. Last night. The angel told me."

Gabriel froze. His eyes widened in awe and disbelief. His gaze darted from Nathan's face to Tyler's broken leg under the blankets, then back to Nathan.

"You… can?" Gabriel breathed.

Tyler's eyes shot open. "No way."

Nathan grinned softly. "Yes way."

Gabriel choked on a laugh, half-threatening to cry. "Nathan, if this is true—"

"It is."

Nathan straightened, lifting his hands over Tyler's body like a priest readying a blessing.

"Um… Doc?" Nathan said politely.

The surgeon looked up, startled. "Yes?"

"I don't think we're going to need surgery today. Or tomorrow. Or—honestly—ever."

The surgeon blinked. "I'm sorry?"

Nathan inhaled deeply.

And heaven answered.

"In the mighty name of Jesus Christ," Nathan declared, voice steady and fierce, "and by the authority of Father God Almighty, and with the blessing of the Holy Spirit, I command these bones to reset and knit together. I command muscle to regrow. I command tissue to renew. And I command all damage to disappear—right now."

He whispered the final word:

"Amen."

A brilliant glow burst from Nathan's hands— warm, radiant, pulsing like living sunlight.

It poured into Tyler's body, sinking into broken bone, torn muscle, bruised tissue. Tyler gasped—not from pain, but from warmth, from wholeness, from a sensation like being remade from the inside out.

The surgeon stumbled backward, nearly dropping his instruments.

"What—what—what is—?!" he stammered.

Tyler sat up.

Just sat up. Easily. Freely. Without pain.

He rotated his wrist. Flexed his ankle. Bent his knee. The movement was effortless, fluid, perfect.

He wiggled his toes, grinning.

Then he punched the air and laughed loudly. "Papa Nathan! You could've asked God for bigger muscles, you know!"

Nathan smirked. "In due time, Tyler. You have to earn those."

Gabriel covered his face with one hand, overcome with trembling relief. He pulled them both into his arms—their healed boy and his miraculous husband—and held them so tightly they almost couldn't breathe.

The surgeon stood there, jaw slack, eyes enormous.

Nathan turned gently to him.

"Doctor… what you saw today was for your unbelief and must remain between us. It is not yet time for this truth to spread. Swear it."

The surgeon swallowed, still visibly shaking. "I… I swear it. Before heaven and earth."

Nathan nodded. "Thank you."

By midday, word of Tyler's survival had spread through the tribal grounds—not the miraculous healing detail; the surgeon kept his oath—but the boy's recovery and courage.

Six to seven dozen members of the returning lineage gathered outside the great pavilion. They were building a new civilization with their hands, stone by stone, but nothing stopped them from pausing their labors when the council called for assembly.

Tonight was not a meeting.

It was a celebration.

Torches lit the perimeter. Drums echoed in warm rhythms. Food simmered over open fires. Children ran barefoot through the grass.

When Tyler approached—walking with a slight stiffness but no pain—the crowd erupted in cheers.

Not out of spectacle. Not from curiosity. But relief. Joy. Love for the heir whose survival meant the continuation of the prophecy they had returned for.

Gabriel lifted Tyler onto the stone platform so everyone could see him.

Nathan stood close beside them, one arm wrapped protectively around his husband.

An elder stepped forward, his voice carrying across the gathered crowd.

"We honor the boy who lived," he proclaimed. "We honor the fathers who saved him. And we honor the God who healed him."

Tyler's cheeks burned with a deep flush. For the first time since the visions had begun, his gaze fell in true humility.

Nathan gave his shoulder a gentle, steadying squeeze, then stepped forward. He lifted both hands toward heaven before lowering himself to his knees in worship and thanksgiving for God's boundless mercies, His miraculous healings, and His steadfast love for these many people.

One by one, then in waves, the entire assembly followed. Men, women, and children sank to their knees in unison, eyes closed, hands raised heavenward. Soft whispers of prayer and praise rose like incense, filling the air with quiet adoration.

Speaking for them all, Nathan raised his voice in prayer.

"Thank You, YAHWEH, for supplying every need even before we know to ask. You have been so good, so faithful to those who serve You. You are always perfectly timed—never too early, never too late—when we need You most. Bless these Your people who kneel with me now in offering You honor and devotion. Pour out miracles upon them as well, in answer to their humility and steadfast dedication."

The words were unscripted, yet they flowed from Nathan as naturally as conversation with a beloved friend standing close— intimate, earnest, and full of purpose. The final "Amen" hung softly in the air, met by a profound, reverent silence as peace settled over the assembly like a gentle mantle.

Nathan rose slowly, his face glowing with a wide, radiant smile.

"Go now," he called, his voice warm and brimming with joy, "and enjoy the feast!"

The people rose as one, their cheers bursting forth like a wave. Laughing and talking, they streamed toward the tables, hearts full and ready to share in the wondrous meal.

The tribe recorded the event—documentation for their growing archives. Preparations for the evening feast began—roasted meats, vegetables grown in newly blessed soil, sweet breads baked by the women who had arrived only days earlier.

The air throbbed with celebration.

But inside, Tyler was quieter.

Not troubled. Not afraid. Just thoughtful.

He still didn't understand the future. He still didn't like what he'd seen. But… he was no longer drowning in it.

Both of his fathers loved him. The angel had spoken truth over him. He knew now that destiny wasn't a chain pulling him into darkness—but a path he would walk with help.

Slowly. Carefully. Maturing into the weight that would one day fit him.

He looked at his fathers, Gabriel laughing with an ancestor, Nathan accepting thanks from a family who had been praying for Tyler's recovery and Nathan pointed to the heavens to redirect the thanks to God.

A soft smile touched his lips.

I'm not alone, he thought. *And I won't face any of this alone.*

And for the first time since the vision that broke him… Tyler felt hope.

(8) The First Three Gauntlets of the Heir

The council chamber loomed older today, its unfinished stone pillars casting jagged shadows that seemed to whisper of forgotten burdens. The air hung thick with the scent of aged wood and earth, unchanged in structure yet transformed by the ancient boxes on the central table—relics dusted with centuries, their leather straps frayed by the touch of countless heirs who had come before. Tyler's heart thudded heavily in his chest, a drumbeat of unease that echoed the room's newfound gravity. *What if I'm not enough? What if this breaks me before I even begin?*

Nathan, Gabriel, and Tyler settled into their seats at the head of the gathering, the curved benches filled with elders whose murmurs wove through the air like threads of lost tongues. Tyler's fathers flanked him, their presence a silent anchor, but even they shifted slightly, sensing the shift from communal warmth to solemn trial.

The eldest historian, silver braids gleaming like moonlight on ancient rivers, unlocked the largest chest with deliberate reverence. A plume of dust swirled upward, catching the morning light in scattered gold. "These," she intoned, her rasping voice carrying the weight of generations, "are the surviving records of the Gauntlet of the Heir."

Tyler's fingers curled into fists, nails biting into slick palms. Nathan leaned in slightly. "Breathe, son," he murmured, low enough for only Tyler and Gabriel to hear. "We're right here."

The plates glowed faintly as she laid them out, symbols spiraling in haunting familiarity. "Every heir before the scattering faced these," she continued, eyes piercing. "Not for strength alone, but to forge the heart, the mind, the spirit. Listen well, young one. These are not stories. They are the path."

She began with the first, voice dropping into a cadence almost like chant.

The Trial of Endurance. "The body must outlast the desert itself. You will carry stones heavier than your own weight across sands that burn the soles and steal the breath. Water—one skin, no more. Then vigils on cliffs where the wind cuts like knives, nights so cold the stars seem to freeze. And the march—three suns rising and setting without rest, without sleep. Many collapse. The strong return with their burden unbroken to the sacred fire." She paused, fixing Tyler with her gaze. "This proves you can carry the people's suffering as your own."

Tyler swallowed, throat dry. "Three days… without sleep?" His voice came out smaller than he intended.

The historian nodded once. "Or more, if the sun demands it."

Gabriel's hand found Tyler's under the table, squeezing gently. "You've got iron in you, Ty. I've seen it."

But Tyler's mind raced: *Iron? I feel like glass right now.*

The Trial of Insight. The elders leaned forward as she spoke more softly, almost reverently. "This is the labyrinth of the soul. Mirrors will show you futures that never were—glory, ruin, your fathers gone. Voices will speak in the dark, half-truths from mouths you trust. Riddles from figures who change faces. Visions of memory and prophecy twisted together. One wrong choice, and you wander forever. This is not cleverness, child. This is the eye of the spirit seeing what the mind cannot."

Tyler felt his pulse spike. "So… it's like being trapped in a nightmare, but you have to find the real door?"

"Precisely," she answered, a faint, approving curve to her lips. "And the nightmare knows your fears best."

Nathan's jaw tightened. He didn't speak, but Tyler could feel the protective tension radiating from him.

The Trial of Devotion. The historian's tone softened further, almost tender. "Here the heir vanishes into the shadow. Weeks may pass in unseen service—tending the fevered in silence, mending roofs beneath starlight, harvesting fields at midnight with bleeding hands, comforting the dying without a word of thanks permitted. Your name is forbidden. Your reward is withheld. We watch, unseen. Bitterness seeps in like poison, corroding the heart. But joy in hidden love—love offered purely for its own sake—purifies it utterly."

She looked directly at Tyler. "This is the trial that reveals the ruler you will become. Will you serve for glory, or because the people are worth more than yourself?"

Tyler stared at the plate, voice barely audible. "I… I want to be that kind of person. But what if I can't? What if I get angry, or tired, or… selfish?"

For the first time, the historian's expression warmed, just a fraction. "That question, child, is the beginning of the answer."

The other elders murmured soft agreement, a ripple of sound like wind through dry grass.

Tyler swallowed again, the lump like gravel. These three trials alone felt like monoliths—too vast, too crushing. Failure whispered horrors: dishonor, delay, or the stripping away of heirship forever. His palms were damp; his chest constricted, breath shallow.

Nathan's steady hand settled on his shoulder, warm and firm. "You're not facing this alone, Tyler. Not one step."

Gabriel leaned closer, voice quiet but fierce. "We've got your back. Every single day of training, every doubt— we're in it with you."

Tyler managed a shaky nod, drawing a breath that felt like pulling air through a straw. The elders closed the first chest with a resonant thud, deferring the rest to tomorrow.

He excused himself after the session, legs heavy, and sought the sacred spring. Sitting alone, he stared into the rippling water, his reflection wavering. *Endurance that could kill me. Insight that could unravel my mind. Devotion that demands my everything.* The first three gauntlets pressed like the stones themselves, their significance mirroring his deepest fears: this was rebirth, the forging of a vessel for a nation. Yet in the quiet, amid the fear, a faint stirring remained—a fragile seed of calling, waiting for water.

(9) The Gauntlet of the Heir – The Final Trials and the Promise

The next morning dawned with a crisp edge, the council chamber now humming with unspoken tension, as if the stones themselves anticipated the climax. Tyler's sleep had been fitful, haunted by dreams of crumbling under unseen weights, his father's faces fading into dust. He returned flanked by Nathan and Gabriel, their presence a bulwark against the rising tide of apprehension. The historian, her silver braids catching the light like threads of fate, opened the second chest without delay, her voice steady but infused with the gravity of what lay ahead. Tyler's thoughts churned: *If the first three were mountains, what horrors await in the last?* The air felt denser, charged with the significance of completion—this was the forge's final hammer strikes, shaping or shattering the heir forever.

She proceeded with solemn precision, unveiling the concluding trials, each one delving deeper into the soul's core.

The Trial of Judgment — The elders' narration evoked a courtroom of the spirit, where the heir presided over thorny disputes engineered to rend the heart. Not petty squabbles, but crucibles of ethics: a simulated famine forcing grain allocation between hollow-eyed families and battle-worn guardians, where favoritism could spark rebellion; an inheritance dispute laced with concealed treacheries, demanding truth's scalpel amid familial bonds; a grave offense where law screamed for execution, yet mercy whispered of redemption's possibility. Rendered publicly under elders' scrutiny, judgments were weighed not for flawlessness but equilibrium—justice laced with compassion, authority without arrogance. A single errant verdict could splinter tribal unity, echoing historical fractures that led to the scattering. This trial's profundity lay in its mirror to leadership's essence: the heir as arbiter of fairness, channeling the wisdom of ancient Israelite judges who balanced Torah's rigor with God's grace. Gabriel's gaze held steady encouragement, but Tyler's mind spiraled: *How do I choose when every path wounds? What if my heart leads me wrong?* The fear gnawed, underscoring the trial's weight—a flawed judge could doom the reborn nation to internal strife.

The Trial of the Calling — The room fell to hushed reverence as they described the pinnacle, the sacred culmination. Alone in the ancestral fire's chamber, amid choking smoke and oppressive silence, the heir bared their soul in total surrender. The flame responded as divine oracle: acceptance manifesting in a towering pillar of blue-white luminescence, warm and vital, signifying heaven's endorsement; refusal as flickering embers dying to cold ash, a rejection that might bar the heir eternally. No appeals, no retries—this was the Holy One's unmediated verdict, a ritual rooted in the tribe's primordial covenant, akin to the biblical tests of fire that separated the chosen from the profane. Nathan's hand tightened subtly on Tyler's arm, conveying faith's quiet power. Tyler's breath snagged, a vise around his lungs: *What if the fire rejects me? What if I'm unworthy, and all this ends in darkness?* The significance thrummed like a heartbeat—this wasn't mere approval; it was divine commissioning, the heir's spirit fused with the ancestors' legacy, igniting the path to national revival or extinguishing it.

Tyler's breath escaped in a ragged gasp, the final trials feeling like the precipice of oblivion. The historian then unfurled the ancient parchment with careful hands, its brittle edges crackling like dry leaves, faded ink a ghost of grandeur. "This," she declared, her voice resonant with awe, "is one of the only surviving maps of our original civilization before captivity."

Unrolled, it sprawled immense, dwarfing modern notions—a true empire etched in intricate detail: gleaming cities cradled by engineered waterways that snaked like lifelines, terraced gardens blooming eternally to feed multitudes, vast plazas thrumming with communal life, halls of learning stacked with scrolls of forgotten wisdom, farms sprawling to horizons where the parchment curled in defeat. Roads veined the land like arteries, pulsing with trade; towers hewn into sheer cliffs pierced the skies as observatories; bridges of fused stone and forged metal arched defiantly over chasms. It eclipsed Egypt's pyramids, the Incas' terraces, the Maya's calendars—perhaps outshone them in harmonious ingenuity. Tyler's jaw slackened, a rush of wonder crashing against his fear: *This was us? A people who tamed rivers and stars?*

Gabriel stared, transfixed, his thoughts a whirlwind of reverence for the lost splendor. Nathan whispered, "My God…," his voice cracking with the revelation's holiness, a bridge to his own faith's ancient roots.

The elder nodded, her expression a blend of sorrow and pride. "Our tribe was once among the world's zenith—engineers who bent nature to abundance, scholars unraveling creation's secrets, warriors unbowed, farmers coaxing life from stone. Ancient Israel allied with us; Egypt envied and enslaved us; the world quaked at our shadow. Yet when we scattered… history erased us, a wound that festers still."

Tyler pivoted to his fathers, his voice a fragile breath amid the storm within: "That's… what I'm supposed to help rebuild?" The words carried the weight of impossibility, a boy's shoulders sagging under an empire's ghost.

"Yes," Gabriel murmured, his eyes soft with belief, though laced with his own unspoken doubts.

"I'm not ready," Tyler confessed, raw vulnerability spilling out, tears pricking his eyes—the trials' cumulative dread crystallizing into admission.

Nathan's squeeze on his shoulder was firm, infused with paternal conviction: "You will be." But even he felt the tremor in Tyler's frame, the boy's thoughts a maelstrom of inadequacy against the map's vast significance—a blueprint for resurrection, demanding an heir equal to gods.

By afternoon, the council etched Tyler's path forward, a regimen that transcended education, sculpting a nation from his sinews.

He would train daily in:

- Physical endurance with returning tribes' warriors, forging his body into a vessel of resilience, each sweat-drenched session a step toward embodying the ancestors' unbreakable spirit.

- Historical studies, tracing lineage to pre-Egyptian dawns, immersing in tales that breathed life into the map's faded lines, instilling a profound sense of continuity and loss.

- Societal law and justice, presiding over mock tribunals that mirrored the Trial of Judgment's thorns, honing ethics to prevent history's repeats.

- Leadership etiquette, manners, diplomacy, royal duties—polishing the heir into a beacon of grace, where every gesture signified unity's fragile thread.

- Agricultural systems, engineering, economics—reviving the empire's ingenuity, hands-on with soil and schematics, symbolizing abundance from ashes.

- Spiritual disciplines: prayer, discernment, worship—deepening communion with the Holy One, the trials' true core, where faith transformed fear into purpose.

It was no mere curriculum; it was alchemy, rebuilding an empire within one trembling youth. Tyler exhaled shakily, overwhelmed by the density of expectation—yet a subtle stirring ignited within, a recognition of calling amid the chaos, like a dormant seed sensing rain.

Still, fear wove through his heart, a persistent shadow. He withdrew to the sacred spring's embrace, the water's ripple a soothing counterpoint to his turmoil. Kneeling, the cool earth grounding him, he grappled with prayer's mystery—he'd witnessed Nathan's bold petitions, but his own felt feeble, a whisper in a gale. He felt infinitesimal, a speck against the gauntlet's immensity.

Lifting his eyes to the canopy, leaves filtering dappled light like divine veils, he poured out his soul: "God… I don't know what I'm doing. I'm afraid I'll ruin everything—the trials, the tribe, this legacy. I'm afraid I'll disappoint them, shatter their hopes. I'm afraid… of losing them, my fathers, this fragile family."

The water rippled, as if in empathy.

A warmth enveloped the clearing, soft as a mother's embrace, quiet as dawn's first breath.

A voice resonated—not thunderous, not terrifying, but a gentle wind rustling leaves, echoing in his chest's deepest chambers: "Ask what you desire of Me."

Tyler swallowed, throat tight with awe and humility. He bypassed pleas for power, strength, visions, might, authority— trappings that paled against his heart's true cry.

He whispered, voice cracking: "Give me… wisdom. Wisdom to lead them through these trials. Wisdom to choose right amid judgment's thorns. Wisdom to bring them closer to You, healing the scattered wounds. Wisdom to keep us together, unbreakable."

Tyler knelt there, breath quivering, hands clenched until knuckles whitened like bleached bone. He braced for silence, for nothingness—a mere boy petitioning the Cosmos's Architect for the unattainable.

Yet the air shifted, the very ether leaning in, attentive and intimate.

The voice returned, profound yet tender, settling into his marrow like a father's lullaby: "Your request is honorable, child."

Tyler gasped softly, eyes widening in disbelief, a surge of holy terror and joy mingling.

"You have not asked for power… nor the defeat of enemies… nor the wealth of nations… nor glory for yourself."

Warmth bloomed in his chest, unfurling like dawn's rays piercing ribs, banishing shadows.

"You have asked for wisdom. Wisdom to lead. Wisdom to unify. Wisdom to strengthen what was broken and to bind hearts together again."

Tyler swallowed tears, voice a hoarse whisper: "I… I just want to help them. I want to make the right choices. I don't want to fail my—Your—people… or my dads… or You."

The presence intensified, not oppressive but enveloping, a luminous blanket of comfort.

"Because you have asked this, Tyler— because your heart bends toward your people rather than yourself—I will bless you."

Before breath could form, creation responded.

A balmy gust swirled through the trees, encircling him, lifting hair and garments in an ethereal embrace—holy, ordered, divine hands cradling the heir.

The earth trembled softly beneath, awakening like a slumbering giant after millennia.

The spring surged, crystalline waters erupting in a shimmering cascade, carving a sinuous channel downhill with architectural precision, as if etched by celestial design.

Soil drank thirstily, parched veins revitalized.

Then the miracle cascaded: verdant shoots erupted in symphony, fruit trees—apple, pear, fig, pomegranate—maturing in moments, blossoms unfurling in fragrant defiance of time. Vines twisted upward, heavy with grapes and lush foliage. Grass swelled in emerald undulations, plush as royal tapestry. Herbs— sage, thyme, lavender—burst forth, perfuming the air with healing scents. Wildflowers splashed the earth in sapphire blues, amethyst violets, sun-kissed golds.

Beyond, visions flickered like prophetic glimpses: fertile farmlands sprawling kingdom-wide, herds proliferating in secure pastures, silos brimming with generational grain, fields verdant through drought's barren kiss, trade routes emerging organically along the river's gift, an economy thriving on plenty's roots rather than want's thorns.

The land hummed with sacred vitality—a covenant inscribed in soil, signifying God's faithfulness to a humbled heir.

Tyler clamped a hand over his mouth, sobs wracking him, overwhelmed by the extravagance: *This... for me? For us?*

The voice thundered softly within: "This river will nourish the people. This land will flourish under your care. Where there was scarcity, there will now be abundance. Where there was wandering, there will now be home. And as long as your heart seeks wisdom, I will sustain you… and those you lead."

The warmth subsided, infusing his essence eternally.

Tyler collapsed forward, tears anointing the nascent grass: "Thank You…" he murmured, gratitude a sacred litany. "Thank You…"

A zephyr caressed his cheek, affirming: "Rise, young heir. Your journey has begun."

Tyler rose unsteadily, beholding the transfigured vista—vibrant, pulsating with life, impossibly resplendent. God hadn't merely answered; He'd overflowed, sealing significance in every leaf: a boy's humble plea birthing a nation's renewal.

By dusk, the great hall brimmed with life, torches flickering amber across assembled faces—elders etched with time's wisdom, historian's guardians of lore, engineer's dreamers of stone, warriors scarred sentinels, families newly reunited in hope's fragile glow. Incense wafted from the central censer, sweet and resinous, evoking ancient altars, infusing the air with ceremony's solemnity.

This night transcended gatherings; it was witness to divinity's footprint.

Tyler sat between his fathers—Nathan's quiet strength to his left, Gabriel's warm steadiness to his right—his hands quivering not from terror now, but awe's aftershocks, a profound shift from doubt to anointed purpose.

The chief elder, braids cascading like wisdom's cascade, eyes deep as ancient wells, unfurled a scroll more venerable than standing structures: "We convene for two divine imperatives: the land's benediction and a man's consecration."

Murmurs of reverence rippled, hearts attuned to the sacred.

He addressed Tyler first: "Boy heir, word reaches us of your plea for wisdom from the Almighty."

Tyler nodded, swallowing nerves, glancing to Nathan for bolstering—his father's nod a silent *You've got this*.

"And it was granted."

Tyler rose, small yet resolute, voice soft but threaded with newfound conviction: "I asked for wisdom—not strength, not power, nothing for me alone. To help the tribe, lead justly, draw us nearer to God."

Elders inclined their heads, touched by the echo of Solomon's plea, hearts stirring with ancestral resonance.

"And in asking," Tyler continued, cheeks flushing with humility's heat, "the land responded. God overflowed the spring into a river. Plants surged, trees fruited instantly. The earth awoke." He averted his eyes: "I expected nothing. I just wanted… to honor everyone."

The chief raised hands in veneration: "This heralds divine favor upon tribe and heir. The God of Israel renews our covenant. Abundance is no chance; it's promise reborn."

Tears flowed freely; prayers murmured in tongues of yore; palms pressed to chests in grateful acknowledgment.

He then unveiled the second scroll, fragile as memory: "The Prophecy of the Foreign Fire, preserved from pre-captivity epochs."

He recited, words soaring like liturgy: "A man not of our line shall come. A bearer of foreign fire. Clothed in white, marked by heaven, he will walk with God and teach His ways. He will bless the scattered ones, guide the heir, and light the path back to the Holy One. His flame will not consume, but purify, restore, and unite. Through him the tribe shall learn the ways of Jesus the Messiah and the wisdom of the ancients who walked with God in Israel."

The prophecy hung, resonant as a sacred hymn, every gaze pivoting to Nathan.

He felt Gabriel's hand entwine his, a tether of love amid the surge.

Tyler's heart expanded, pride and reverence swelling for his father.

The chief lowered the scroll: "Foreign Fire, radiant with God's essence. Teacher, guardian, white-clad. Nathan… from your arrival, we sensed it."

Nathan inclined his head, voice hushed with humility: "I am only a servant." Thoughts flooded him—*Me? Chosen? Yet it fits, this fire within, kindled by grace.*

The elder smiled: "As all the elects are." Then, deepening the wonder: "The prophecy omits healing, yet it flows from you— overflowing favor, proof of God's extravagant love for this tribe."

The tribal surgeon advanced, trembling with witnessed glory, bowing profoundly: "I testify: not medicine, not science—divine miracle."

Hand over heart, voice fracturing: "Tyler's leg shattered, arm fractured twice, tissues ravaged. No mortal mends in instants."

Council edged closer, breaths held.

"But Nathan invoked God, and light infused the boy. Bones knit seamlessly. Flesh renewed. Bruises evaporated. Instantaneous. Holy." He bowed anew: "I vow this before heaven and Earth."

Stunned hush yielded to gasps, praise shouts, elders' upraised hands, and a woman kneeling in joyful sobs.

Nathan advanced, core humbled: *This gift given to me comes from God so all may see Him move among His people.*

The chief queried: "Nathan, do you claim this?"

Nathan bowed: "I acknowledge, but it's God's alone."

"And will you wield it for the tribe?"

"For all in need, as He guides," Nathan affirmed, voice steady with purpose.

The hall ignited: drums thrummed ancient holy cadences, feet rose, hands ascended, voices chanted praises etched in blood memory. The council bowed—not to Nathan, but the indwelling Fire.

Nathan's eyes glistened with tears unshed, overwhelmed by destiny's weave.

Gabriel's touch on his shoulder beamed pride and awe.

Tyler beheld his fathers—one the prophesied Fire, one the warrior-pillar—and himself, the wisdom-blessed heir. Realization dawned: their fates intertwined, a trinity forged for rebirth. Not separate strands, but a family's sacred braid, signifying hope's triumph over scattering—a nation rising from humble prayers and divine flames.

(10) Moving Forward, Unifying the Grounds of the Land

With morale surging, the tribe returned to work with renewed vigor. Their numbers grew weekly with insurgences of tribe members coming back, summoned by the earth beacon that thumped and called them.

Hundreds of families now worked daily:

- quarrying stone
- carving beams
- shaping bricks
- creating dwellings
- weaving textiles
- tending livestock
- irrigating early crops
- storing crops, grains, and
- operating stores for trade
- mapping infrastructure

Children carried messages between dwellings, tents, campsites, and more. Engineers sketched large-scale plans for the city center. Craftsmen built the first tools of their revived society.

The estate became a living beehive of renewal.

Tyler watched it all with new eyes.

He finally understood:

This wasn't just a tribe. It was a nation. A kingdom coming back to life.

And he was its heir.

At sunrise the next morning, the council gathered again—this time with a sharper urgency beneath their words. The shadows cast by early light stretched long across the table, where maps lay layered like centuries of memories waiting to be retraced.

Digital holograms flickered beside ancient papyrus scrolls. Hand-drawn charts—some thousands of years old—rested beside sleek satellite images. Drones buzzed overhead like metallic insects, scanning the terrain for signs of human settlement.

The tribe had one foot in the ancient world and one in the modern—and it was time to walk forward with both.

"Who will go?"

Nathan stood at the edge of the table, studying a map marked with faded routes that had once belonged to Gabriel's ancestors. The ink was cracked, but the path still pulsed with significance.

Gabriel rested a steady hand on his shoulder. "We'll need more than a few to begin this search."

The chief elder nodded. "Then let us decide who is worthy of the first expedition."

She lifted her staff slightly, pointing to the assembled volunteers—a diverse, formidable group already gathering along the hall's perimeter.

The Warriors

A squad of six elite fighters stepped forward, clad in light armor stitched with ancestral sigils.

- **Karn**, the silent strategist
- **Miro**, agile and sharp-eyed
- **Eliah**, whose family guarded the old histories
- **Ressa**, unmatched in tracking
- **Yadin**, a mountain-born giant
- **Tamar**, fierce, fast, and unshakeable

These were the tribe's best protectors.

"They will defend you," the elder said to Nathan. "Against weather, against danger, and if necessary… against men."

Nathan bowed his head in thanks.

The Scholars

Four historians approached, each carrying tablets and scroll cases.

- **Sereth**, an interpreter of ancient languages
- **Halli**, expert on tribal migrations
- **Talem**, a geographer with encyclopedic memory
- **Naris**, a keeper of stories and oral tradition

"You will need to identify ruins, symbolic carvings, dialect variations," Sereth said. "Your spiritual instincts will guide you, Nathan, but our knowledge will confirm what you find."

The Spiritual Pair

An elderly man and his granddaughter stepped forward.

- **Daro**, the tribe's oldest spiritual discerner
- **Siyah**, a young empath rumored to sense truth in the air

"These two," the chief elder said, "can detect spiritual movement—echoes of the blessing, traces of the lost clans. They will hear what eyes cannot see."

Nathan nodded, recognizing the gravity of such companions.

The Tech Specialists

Three young adults stepped up, wearing sleek gear—drones strapped to their backs, communication devices clipped to belts, augmented-reality scanners glowing faintly.

- **Lenn**, drone pilot
- **Kessa**, engineer
- **Veo**, long-range comm expert

"Technology must stand beside the ancient ways," Gabriel said firmly. "We won't reject progress—not after everything we've learned."

The elder smiled. "Your modern world and our forgotten world can coexist."

Where will they go?

Talem spread a massive parchment across the table. On it, red circles glowed faintly—each marking possible sites of ancestral scattering.

"There are five major routes," he explained:

Route One — The Northern Mountains: Where early refugees fled into icy passes, hiding in deep caverns.

Route Two — The Eastern Deserts: Where nomadic clans may have mixed with desert tribes centuries ago.

Route Three — The Southern Cities: Where descendants likely blended into urban populations, hiding in plain sight.

Route Four — The Western Archipelagos: Where ships vanished during the scattering, possibly forming hidden island communities.

Route Five — The Far Continental Divide: A route so ancient that even the elders only knew fragments—it pointed toward a land across the ocean, where a cluster of symbols matched the ancestral crest.

"There," Naris whispered, "is the most promising. And the most dangerous."

"And that," Gabriel said, "is where Nathan will lead the first team."

Nathan exhaled slowly. It wasn't fear he felt—just the weight of calling. A sacred burden.

Tyler looked at him with widening eyes. "You're really going out there?"

Nathan smiled gently. "Someone must go first."

How will they get there?

Kessa activated a holographic projection of vehicles.

"Our team will travel by hybrid transport:

- ground rovers for mountains

- desert crawlers for dunes
- air skimmers for the archipelagos
- and long-range jets for crossings."

Nathan raised a brow. "We have jets?"

Gabriel smirked. "We do now. The tribe acquired them while you were healing Tyler."

Nathan groaned softly. "I sleep for five hours, and you people start an airline."

Tyler burst out laughing.

But then Gabriel's expression turned serious.

"Transportation is covered. But we need to talk about safety."

What about safety?

Ressa, the tracker, stepped forward.

"We use layered protection. Physical, technological, and spiritual."

She pointed to each in turn:

Physical - Warriors guarding every flank, with rotating night watches.

Technological:

- Drones scouting ahead
- Thermal scanners
- Encryption-protected comms
- Emergency locators

Spiritual - Daro lifted his staff.

"We will pray daily. Your path will be shielded. No force of darkness will cross us uninvited."

Nathan felt warmth stir in his chest—the same voice from the spring whispering reassurance.

Finally, the chief elder addressed the room.

"This journey will be long. Dangerous. But necessary. The tribe cannot be whole until the scattered are gathered. And as the prophecy says—the Foreign Fire must go first."

Nathan bowed his head, accepting the mantle.

Tyler stared at him—fear, pride, and awe mingling in his expression.

Nathan reached over and squeezed his shoulder.

"This is the beginning," Nathan said softly.

Tyler swallowed. "Of destiny?"

Nathan nodded. "Of everything."

(11) Paths That Divide – The Sending and the Farewell

The sun rose like a slow-burning ember over the valley, its golden rays spilling across the awakening tribe like a divine promise, illuminating faces etched with a mix of reverence and quiet sorrow. Hundreds gathered outside the great pavilion, lining the broad stone platform that served as the ceremonial grounds—a place steeped in ancient memory, where the earth itself seemed to hum with the echoes of past departures. Today was not a feast day nor a tribal festival; it was a sending, a sacred act older than the tribe's forgotten empire, rooted in rituals that bound the living to the ancestors and the scattered to the homeward call. Drums throbbed low and rhythmically, their beats mimicking the pulse of a reluctant heart, drawing the crowd into a shared breath of anticipation and loss.

Nathan stood at the center of the circle, dressed in ceremonial white—not gaudy, not extravagant, but pure, clean, reverent, exactly as the prophecy described the Foreign Fire. The fabric caught the light like captured starshine, a visual echo of the divine flame within him. Gabriel helped adjust the mantle draped over Nathan's shoulders, his fingers lingering a heartbeat too long, tracing the seam as if committing the texture to memory. *How can I let him go?* Gabriel thought, his chest tightening with a fear he dared not voice—fear of the unknown paths, the lurking dangers, the possibility that this mantle might one day be all that returned. Tyler stood on Nathan's other side, trying to appear composed, though he kept gripping and releasing his hands to keep them from shaking, his young mind swirling with a storm of emotions: pride in his father's calling, terror at the void it would leave, and a budding understanding of sacrifice's bitter weight.

The elders approached in procession, each carrying an object of symbolic power, their steps measured and solemn, evoking the gravity of ancient initiations where the departed were blessed to bridge worlds:

- A scroll of the tribe's laws, representing the justice they carried forth.
- A vial of water from the holy spring, symbol of life's renewal and purification.
- A torch lit from the ancestral flame, embodying the enduring spirit.
- A small carved stone representing the land, a tangible piece of home to ground the wanderer.

The chief elder stepped forward, her voice carrying across the crowd like wind through sacred groves, infused with the authority of generations. "Foreign Fire," she said, "you are called by God and by prophecy. You are blessed to go forth and seek our scattered kin, to bring home what history stole, to restore what was broken."

Nathan bowed deeply, his heart swelling with humility and resolve, yet laced with the ache of impending separation—a profound exploration of his dual role as servant and father, understanding now more than ever that true calling demanded the surrender of personal anchors.

The elder dipped her fingers in the vial of sacred water and touched Nathan's forehead, the cool droplet tracing a path like a tear unshed. "In the name of the Almighty, walk with courage."

Another placed the carved stone in his hand, its rough edges pressing into his palm like a reminder of the earth's unyielding strength. "In memory of the homeland you restore."

Another held out the torch, its flame flickering with warmth that mirrored the fire in his soul. "For the fire that burns within you."

Then one more stepped out—an unexpected figure. Tyler. He held nothing in his hands—only his heart shining openly through his eyes, wide with the raw vulnerability of a boy on the cusp of manhood, grappling with the depth of love and the fear of loss.

He stepped toward Nathan, voice trembling like a thin wire. "Papa Nathan… come home. Okay?"

Nathan cupped Tyler's cheek with a tenderness that rooted the entire crowd into silence, his thumb brushing away an invisible tear, his own eyes misting as memories flooded him—of Tyler's broken body healed, of shared prayers by the spring, of a family forged in divine fire. He drew him into a full embrace—fierce, warm, anchoring, the kind that spoke volumes without words, exploring the unbreakable bond that transcended distance. When he pulled back, he handed the ceremonial torch off to his armor-bearer with a quiet, "Hold this for me, please."

And then, without warning, Nathan swept Tyler into his arms and zoomed like a rocket upward into the atmosphere, but not too high, the rush of wind whipping around them like a whirlwind of emotion.

Gasps rippled through the tribe as both father and son soared high above the gathering—so high the people below looked like clusters of earth-colored dots, a visual reminder of the vastness of their world and the smallness of individual lives within it.

Tyler yelped in surprise, arms snapping tight around Nathan's neck. "Papa—! We're—this is—this is really high!"

Nathan chuckled softly, keeping him secure, his laughter a balm against the height's terror, yet his own heart pounded with the weight of this moment—an exploration of legacy, passing the torch even as he prepared to leave. "Look down, sweetheart. Tell me what you see."

Tyler swallowed hard and forced himself to peek over Nathan's shoulder, his fear giving way to awe as the valley unfolded like a living tapestry. "I see… a bunch of people," he whispered, his voice small but gaining strength, beginning to understand the broader significance of his role.

Nathan's voice warmed, laced with paternal pride and a touch of sorrow. "Exactly. But when I look down, I see you first. I see the one who will lead them long after I'm gone. I see their future. Their hope."

Tyler blinked rapidly, throat tightening, tears pricking as he internalized the words—a profound realization of his inheritance, not just of title but of responsibility, feeling the mantle's weight settle on his young shoulders.

"And then," Nathan continued, "I see your people—your tribe— who will need you every bit as much as you'll discover you need them."

The wind tugged gently at Tyler's hair as Nathan went on: "As you rise into authority, as you grow into the man God designed you to be, you'll take your Dad's place one day. And when that happens, you'll need to exhibit all he is… and all God expects of you."

Tyler pressed his forehead into Nathan's shoulder, overwhelmed, his mind racing through flashes of doubt and determination, exploring the depths of his calling amid the fear of inadequacy.

Nathan kissed the crown of his head. "Now… while I'm gone? Please don't break any more bones." He softened it with a smirk. "And if you do—channel me. You can reach me, Tyler. I already speak telepathically with your Dad across long distances, and I'm working on that link with you too. You know how to find me. Alright?"

Tyler nodded into his chest, the promise anchoring him, fostering a deeper understanding of their spiritual connection beyond physical presence.

Nathan held him tighter, then slowly descended. They landed with a soft, controlled stomp that sent a faint tremor through the ground, symbolizing the impact of their bond on the tribe.

The tribe erupted into awed whispers, murmurs of "The Foreign Fire flies!" rippling like prayers, their collective reverence deepening the moment's significance.

Nathan lifted his hand, and a pulse of brilliant light swept outward, enveloping everyone gathered, a warm embrace from the divine that stirred souls and eased fears. When he spoke, his voice rolled like thunder: "God be with you as you follow Him. Be still… and recognize who He is."

The light swelled once more—then vanished, leaving a lingering peace that explored the tribe's faith, reminding them of God's omnipresence amid separation.

Nathan brushed a tear from Tyler's cheek. "I will try too, Tyler. God willing, I'll come home. And I'll bring back more of our people."

Tyler's chin trembled as he nodded, his heart aching with love and uncertainty.

Gabriel stepped forward, breath uneven as he placed a steadying hand on Nathan's shoulder, his touch a silent plea amid his internal turmoil—exploring the fragility of their partnership, understanding that love's strength lay in release. "Just… be careful," he whispered.

Nathan leaned their foreheads together, a quiet, sacred gesture, their breaths mingling in shared vulnerability. "Always."

His armor-bearer approached, offering the ceremonial torch and flame.

"Just beyond the eastern cavern," Gabriel said, voice steadier now, though his eyes betrayed the storm within, "you'll find the jets. Load up and use your voice to command the bots. I've programmed all the maps and names."

Nathan raised a brow, surprise flickering. Gabriel answered with a faint smirk, as if to say, *Yes, really—the bots are flying this division,* a moment of levity amid the gravity, underscoring their deep understanding.

Then the drums shifted—deep, rising, ancient, a call to depart that resonated in every chest like the inevitability of fate.

Rovers ignited, their engines humming with mechanical life. Drones lifted into synchronized formation, whirring like guardians. Warriors secured their gear, faces set with determination. Scholars gathered their scrolls, eyes alight with purpose. The spiritual guides raised their staffs, invoking silent blessings.

Nathan stepped toward the expedition, his white mantle catching the morning light like living fire, each step an exploration of faith's demands, understanding the profound cost of obedience.

He turned one last time—memorizing his family, his tribe, his home, his gaze lingering on Gabriel and Tyler with a depth that conveyed unspoken volumes of love and resolve.

And then... He walked forward. He lifted a hand—the ceremonial flaming torch raised high. And the tribe bowed in unison, a wave of reverence that honored the moment's sacredness.

The journey had begun.

Nathan boarded the lead rover, and with a rising whir of engines, the convoy began moving down the valley trail. The drones soared above like metallic birds, scanning ahead in precise sweeps, the dust cloud trailing like a farewell shroud.

Gabriel and Tyler stood on the ridge overlooking the departure path, the wind carrying faint echoes of the drums. Tyler clutched the railing until his knuckles whitened, his mind a whirlwind of what-ifs, exploring the void Nathan's absence carved. "Dad… what if he doesn't come back?"

Gabriel swallowed hard, his gaze locked on the shrinking procession, the dust drifting behind them like a veil, his own fears mirroring Tyler's—separation's cruel blade. "He will," Gabriel said—but his voice was softer than intended, a little too strained, revealing the cracks in his resolve.

Tyler looked up at him sharply. "You're scared too."

Gabriel didn't deny it. He couldn't. Instead, he wrapped an arm around Tyler's shoulders, pulling him close, their shared warmth a bulwark against the chill of uncertainty. "Being scared doesn't mean God won't protect him. It just means he matters."

Tyler leaned into him, drawing comfort from the embrace, beginning to understand fear's role in deepening love.

"He said he saw something… that he wouldn't finish the journey. Not all the way."

Gabriel closed his eyes, pain flickering behind them, exploring the prophecy's shadows. "I know. And that's why we pray."

"Will it be enough?"

Gabriel placed a kiss on Tyler's hair, holding him tighter, his voice steadying with faith's quiet assurance. "It has to be."

Below them, the rovers disappeared beyond the ridge, leaving only echoes and the ache of parting.

A mere hour into the expedition, the terrain shifted into rugged foothills—a place where the earth folded into jagged ridges and wind carved patterns through stone, evoking the tribe's ancient trials of endurance. The team advanced in staggered formation, the air thick with dust and determination, when a piercing cry rang out up ahead.

"Stop the rover!" Nathan shouted, his voice cutting through the rumble like a command from on high.

A warrior named Eliah pointed toward a collapsed cliff edge, his face paling. A young scout—barely sixteen, eyes wide with shock—had misjudged the slope and tumbled down. His leg bent at a sickening angle, breath shallow, face pale with pain and fear, the injury a stark reminder of the journey's perils.

Nathan sprinted toward him, his white robes billowing like wings, his mind flashing to Tyler's own healing—exploring the divine gift's purpose in moments like this, understanding it as a bridge between prophecy and humanity.

The others rushed to secure the perimeter, expecting Nathan to call for medical supplies, their movements hurried yet reverent.

Instead, Nathan knelt beside the boy, placing a hand on his chest and another on his shattered limb, feeling the pulse of life and broken bone beneath his fingers.

"Nathan—wait!" Miro called, urgency in his tone. "We have equipment, we can—"

Nathan shook his head, his focus unwavering, delving into faith's depths. "God," he whispered, voice trembling with humility and power, "You healed my son. Heal this child."

A soft glow emanated from his palms. The air warmed, charged with holy energy. The injured boy gasped as bone corrected itself, muscle stitching back together, skin smoothing as though the injury had been a fading memory, the miracle evoking awe and a deeper understanding of God's overflowing grace.

Moments later, the boy sat up—breathing, whole, stunned, his eyes reflecting newfound reverence.

"You're… you're the one from the prophecy," he whispered, voice laced with wonder.

Nathan helped him stand, steadying him with a gentle grip. "I'm just His servant. It's God who healed you."

The team bowed their heads in reverence, the moment fostering a collective exploration of faith's immediacy, understanding their leader as a vessel of the divine.

And the journey continued, the healed scout's steps a testament to the path's sacred purpose.

With the boy safe, they hurried back toward the edge of the caverns, where the clearing opened to the launch platform. Their jets were already humming—sleek, compact craft built for navigating the fifth and most ancient route, the one no modern traveler touched without a blessing or a death wish, its mysteries stirring a mix of excitement and trepidation.

Gabriel checked the coordinates telepathically, his voice echoing in Nathan's mind with concern. "The route has shifted slightly. Storm activity along the upper corridor. But it still leads to the waypoint marked on the old parchment."

"Then that's where we go," Nathan replied, his resolve firm, understanding the route as a metaphor for faith's unpredictable turns.

They boarded, engines ignited, and the squad shot skyward—
through mist, through towering ridges, through the thinning
breath of ancient air, each ascent a step deeper into the unknown,
laden with feeling and the profound exploration of destiny's call.

(12) Paths That Begin – Revelations and Forging Anew

Hours later the jets followed those glowing ancient threads—faint, shimmering lines that looked like the ancestors themselves were guiding them. They dropped into a narrow valley tucked deep between sharp mountain ridges. No modern map showed it, but their old parchment had marked the spot in faded ink. The air hit them first: clean, cold, smelling of fresh dirt, pine, and something else—electric, almost alive. The ground itself seemed to hum under their feet, like it remembered the old empire, the shamans who used to call down fire and blood to speak with the gods, back when the world was young and wild.

Talem stepped out first. His boots sank a little into the soft earth, like the valley was sizing him up. "This is it," he said quietly, almost to himself. "The place the old writings called the remnant's meeting ground. Where everything was supposed to come together again."

The silence was thick. Even the wind felt like it was watching, deciding whether they belonged.

Elder Daro lifted his staff—old thunderwood, carved generations ago when the first elders sealed pacts with the sky—and sniffed the air. "Something's waking up down there," he said, voice low and rough. "Old power. It's been sleeping for a long time."

A shiver ran through the group. For a second Daro's eyes went distant, like he could see the ghosts of shamans chanting around fires, whispering about a stranger who would bring flame and open the way.

They sent up the drones. The little machines buzzed like curious insects, their scans flickering and fighting the strange energy before finally locking on one spot: a perfect circle of ground that pulsed, slow and steady, like a heartbeat that didn't belong to anything natural.

Nathan felt it before he saw it—a tug deep in his chest, warm and sure, the same pull he'd felt at the spring when the water came alive. He walked toward the circle, boots crunching softly. "This is the place," he said simply. No doubt in his voice.

One of the warriors stepped forward without a word and offered his sword. The blade was old, etched with symbols no one fully understood anymore. Nathan took it, knelt, and began carving a wide circle in the dirt. The metal sang faintly against the soil, almost eager, like it recognized the old rite.

When the circle closed, he drove the point into the center and stood. He raised his right hand. The air grew heavy, tasting faintly of metal and storm.

Light gathered in his palm—soft at first, then brighter, warmer. A flame bloomed, steady and alive, carrying the same quiet power as the prayers he'd whispered in the dark.

He let it go.

The fire shot down, traced the circle in a perfect ring of light, then sank into the earth like it was being pulled through a door only it could see. Heat rolled off the ground in waves. For a heartbeat everything was still—then the valley answered.

A low groan came up through the dirt. The earth shook, not violently, just enough to make your stomach drop. Stone pushed upward, soil sliding away like water, revealing an arch—clean, whole, untouched by time. Symbols along its curve glowed soft orange, like coals that had never quite gone out.

The shaking stopped. The arch stood there, solid and patient, as if it had been waiting centuries for exactly this moment.

Talem unfolded the parchment with shaking hands. "Nathan… look."

The ink was moving. Lines that had been faint sharpened. Places that had been blank filled in. And right in the center, a new mark appeared: the arch, drawn fresh, matching the one in front of them perfectly.

Daro stared, breathing slowly. "The old scrolls… they were waiting for the door to open."

Then Talem's wrist unit beeped. The digital map on the screen redrew itself—satellite lines shifting, elevation numbers changing, a little alert popping up: "Uncharted geological feature detected." Modern tech quietly admitted it had been wrong, making room for something older.

Nathan rested his hand on the warm stone. It pulsed in time with his heartbeat. The glowing words along the arch came clear: *To the one who carries the fire—seek the children of the Western Wind. They remember.*

Talem let out a long breath. "The maps are lining up with the prophecy. This is our road now."

They stood there a moment longer, looking at the arch, feeling the weight of it: a path opening, a world quietly rearranging itself to match an old promise.

Back at the village, night had fallen. Cool wind moved through the torches. Stars came out sharp and bright overhead. Tyler stood in the training yard in his new heir's clothes—light white fabric with green trim from the sacred spring, still feeling strange against his skin.

Three masters waited for him: Ryon with his scarred arms and gravel voice, Ilhera whose eyes saw straight through you, and Janek who carried the calm weight of someone who'd had to make hard calls.

Ryon walked a slow circle around him. "You're the heir. Doesn't mean anything here. You start at the bottom like everyone else. You ready?"

Tyler took a deep breath, still tasting the ache of saying goodbye to Nathan. "Yeah. I'm ready."

They didn't go easy.

Push-ups until his arms burned and the gravel bit into his palms. Laps around the yard until his lungs felt like fire and memories of Nathan's visage taking off flashed behind his eyes. Riddles and puzzles while his head spun from exhaustion. Standing blindfolded, trying to feel the wind's direction, listening for things most people never hear. And finally the hard one, from Janek, when Tyler could barely stand straight: "Two families both swear God promised them the same piece of land. What do you do?"

Tyler wiped sweat from his eyes. "I… listen to both sides. Really listen. Then I pray. I ask for wisdom. I try to find a way they can both live in harmony."

Janek gave the smallest nod. "That's a start."

Ilhera stepped close and laid a hand over his chest. "Fear's still in there, clouding everything. Let it go, child."

Her touch was warm. Something inside Tyler loosened—just a little—and for the first time since the farewell he felt like he could breathe deeper.

When it was finally over, he dropped onto the cool grass, chest heaving, sweat shining in the torchlight. Every muscle hurt, but something else was awake inside him too.

Ryon crouched beside him. "You did well, kid."

Tyler managed a tired smile, wiping his forehead with the back of his hand. "Dad always told me passion matters more than power."

Ryon gave a rare, small grin. "Then you're already stronger than you know."

Tyler tilted his head back, gazing at the scatter of stars overhead, wondering which ones were watching over Nathan right now. "God," he whispered into the cool night air, "please keep him safe."

Far across the mountains, Nathan paused mid-step and glanced back in the direction of home. A quiet warmth brushed across his shoulders—like a prayer had traveled the miles and come to rest right there. It was a small, steady reminder: they were still bound together, no matter how many ridges and valleys stretched between them.

He lowered himself to one knee on the cool stone, the archway's faint glow behind him, and bowed his head. "Lord," he prayed softly, "watch over my family back home. They're carrying heavy things right now—hard days, hard choices. Give them the strength to keep running the race You've set before them. Keep their hearts willing, their spirits open, so when the mountains rise in their path, they'll call on Your Spirit to move them. Amen."

He stayed there a moment longer, letting the silence hold the words, then rose, feeling just a little less alone under the same sky.

As Nathan rose from his knee, the cool night air still clinging to his skin, the faint glow of the archway behind him pulsed once—slow, deliberate, like a heartbeat syncing with his own. He closed his eyes for just a moment longer, and in that quiet space between one breath and the next, the veil thinned.

The vision came gently at first, not overwhelming, but clear as dawn breaking over the ridge.

He saw himself standing on a high overlook, the same valley far below, but transformed. The mountains were crowned with soft golden light, and the archway—now part of a greater circle of ancient stones that had risen in harmony—stood at the center of a gathering. People streamed toward it from every direction: his tribe in their ceremonial whites and greens, faces lit with quiet pride; descendants of the Western Wind, strong and weathered, carrying woven banners that fluttered like living flames; even strangers from distant places, modern clothes mixed with old symbols, drawn by the same pull he had felt.

At the heart of it all stood Tyler—taller now, shoulders broad from trials endured, eyes steady with the wisdom he'd begun to earn. Father and son locked gazes across the distance, and no words were needed. A bridge of warm, shimmering light stretched between them, not fragile but unbreakable, carrying every prayer, every whispered encouragement, every shared heartbeat.

The scene widened. Children laughed and ran through the grass, their voices mingling with the low chant of elders renewing old songs. Fires burned bright but peacefully, and above it all, the stars seemed closer, as if the heavens themselves were leaning in to witness the restoration. The Western Wind moved gently through the valley, carrying scents of new growth—sage, pine, rain on stone—and with it came a deep assurance: the children of the remnant would not just survive; they would thrive, their faith a living fire that no shadow could extinguish.

In the vision, Nathan felt a voice—not loud, but certain—whisper through his spirit: *You carried the flame when it was only embers. Now watch it become a beacon for generations. Your steps were never alone. Keep going. The way is opening.*

The image faded slowly, leaving warmth in his chest and a quiet smile on his face. He touched the arch one last time, fingers tracing the glowing script, then turned toward the path ahead.

Whatever lay next—challenges, unknowns, mountains yet to move—he knew they would face it together, bound by something stronger than distance.

(13) The Children Who Remember – The Call of the Archway

Nathan's POV

The western islands appeared deceptively peaceful on every map we had—clusters of emerald dots scattered across an endless expanse of blue, their jagged outlines almost identical to the ancient sketches etched into the archway's frame. From the air, they looked like fragments of a shattered paradise, carved by relentless wind and time into shapes that whispered of forgotten purpose.

That archway…

It had begun humming at dawn.

A low, resonant vibration rolled through the stone, as a tuning fork struck in another dimension entirely. The sound wasn't loud enough to rattle bones, but it burrowed deep—into muscle, into marrow, into the quiet places of the soul where certainty lives. I stood before it now, alone for a moment, running my fingertips across the symbols that matched the inscription we had uncovered in the valley days earlier:

Seek the children of the Western Wind. They remember.

The stone was warm beneath my touch. Not feverish. Not burning. Just… alive. A subtle heat that pulsed in time with my heartbeat, as though the archway recognized me and was trying, gently, to speak.

This was no mere ornament. No ruined monument left to crumble under vines and salt spray. It wanted to be used.

Not like a Stargate, not a mechanical portal waiting for a dial or a code. More like a compass forged in spirit. A conductor of ancient memory. A spiritual antenna reaching toward the people it once belonged to—people who had carried the same blood, the same songs, the same covenant through centuries of exile.

I closed my eyes and felt it.

A pull. Soft. Insistent. Unwavering.

The archway wasn't meant to let us pass through its frame. It was meant to show us where to go—and who was waiting.

Behind me, the warriors and scholars moved with practiced efficiency, loading gear into two different transports: a mid-range aircraft for distant island landings and a reinforced ocean vessel for navigating the treacherous shallows around volcanic reefs. The air smelled of diesel, salt, and the faint metallic tang of anticipation.

Talem approached, holding a stack of scrolls, his face lined with the quiet intensity of a man who had read too many prophecies and believed every word. "Every map we have aligns with the curvature of these islands," he said, voice low. "If the archway is responding, then the tribe we seek may still hold some variant of the old customs. The rituals. The language. The memory."

"Because they remember," I murmured, the words tasting like prayer.

Talem nodded, eyes flicking back to the archway. "Exactly."

I stared at the structure again, watching how sunlight bent around its edges, as if the air itself respected its age. The symbols along the frame glimmered faintly—not bright, not alarming—just awake. A quiet awakening that stirred something deep inside me, a mix of awe and responsibility that pressed against my ribs.

Miro stepped closer, wiping sweat from his brow. "How does it help us exactly, Commander?"

I answered slowly, letting the truth form in my mind as I felt the archway's pulse sync with my own. "It's a guide. Not a door. It tunes itself to the places where our people still survive."

"Like… a beacon?" Miro asked, brows knitting.

"More like a heartbeat," I replied. "It recognizes its own bloodline."

Silence fell, heavy and reverent, broken only by the distant cry of seabirds.

The archway shifted again—just barely—its glow intensifying at the top and dimming near the base. I traced the pattern with my eyes, feeling the subtle shift in energy.

Gabriel would have understood its rhythm instantly. He always felt the spiritual currents like music. Tyler would have asked a thousand questions, his curiosity a bright flame against the unknown.

But here, with my team, I carried the weight of interpretation alone.

Talem tapped one of the carvings. "This sand-etching—here. It suggests a ritual of alignment. You may be required to activate it again once we reach the island."

My jaw tightened. "Meaning whatever we find… may not want to be found."

Daro, the spiritual elder, stepped forward, his staff sinking slightly into the soft earth. "Or perhaps," he said quietly, his voice carrying the calm of a man who had walked with God through worse, "they are waiting for you."

The words landed like stones in still water. I wasn't sure that was any more comforting.

By mid-morning, we stood on the shoreline, the sea breathing slow pulses against volcanic rock. In the distance, the first island rose from the water like the spine of a sleeping giant, mist clinging to its peaks.

The air tasted of salt, wind, and something older—something that curled into the corners of my mind, stirring echoes of prayers I had prayed in the cavern, of healings I had witnessed, of a family I had left behind.

God, keep them safe while I'm gone.

The team assembled around me:

- Warriors securing weapons and shields, faces set with disciplined focus.
- Scholars cross-checking coastal runes against the archway's inscriptions.
- Tech crew calibrating sonar drones, their screens flickering with data.
- Siyah and Daro stood quietly, heads tilted, listening to the spirit of the place.

The boats tugged at their moorings, eager to cut across the waves. Above us, skimmer-craft whirred to life, ready for aerial reconnaissance.

Miro approached, saluting crisply. "Commander," he said—because out here, away from the estate, away from Gabriel's steady shadow, I was the natural lead, the Foreign Fire. "Do we take the boat or the aircraft first?"

I glanced at the horizon. The archway's pull vibrated faintly through my chest, pointing toward a cluster of islands half-hidden by morning mist.

"Both," I decided. "Boat to approach quietly. Aircraft to scout ahead. We don't know what's waiting on those shores."

"Or who," Siyah added softly, her voice carrying the weight of intuition.

I nodded. "Or who?"

I checked my pack one last time—the carved stone from the sending ceremony, my travel cloak, the small journal Tyler had slipped into my hands before sunrise with a note in his careful handwriting:

Write what you see. Bring the stories home.

I smiled at the memory—Tyler rubbing sleep from his eyes, pretending not to worry, though I had seen the fear in his young face.

The boat crested the final wave and drifted into the shadow of the first island—a towering spire of black volcanic rock split by streams of cascading water. Mist hung thick in the air, threaded with the scent of salt and flowers that didn't exist on the mainland.

I stepped to the bow. My chest tightened.

Something was watching.

Not a person. Not an animal. Something ancient enough to perceive essence rather than shape.

Daro sensed it too. His old eyes narrowed. "Steady," he murmured. "We enter sacred waters."

As the prow breached a ring of smooth stones circling the lagoon, the sea lit up.

A radiant pulse surged beneath the waves, bright as moonlight but shimmering like a thousand tiny fires. It rippled outward in perfect concentric circles, illuminating the depths.

Gasps erupted from the crew.

"What is that—?" Miro whispered, gripping the rail.

But I knew. The water responded to me. To the Foreign Fire.

The glow intensified, forming a luminous path that led toward the inner shore.

Talem choked out, "It's… guiding us."

Daro touched the water reverently. "It is welcoming you. Or warning us what will happen if we turn back."

I didn't hesitate. "Follow it."

The boat glided forward as if drawn by invisible hands. The glowing water parted in a smooth arc, revealing a hidden inlet.

The inlet narrowed into a natural corridor of stone and towering vines. The air thickened, humming with energy.

Karn, the lead warrior, stiffened. "Something's here."

The vines above rustled. Shadows shifted.

Six figures dropped from the trees, surrounding the boat in the shallows—faces masked, torsos painted with ash and indigo, armed with spears carved from volcanic glass.

The team froze.

I lifted my hands slowly. "We come in peace."

The island warriors did not respond.

One—taller, muscles taut, eyes glowing faintly beneath his mask—stepped forward. His spear tip hovered inches from my chest.

He spoke a single word in an ancient dialect.

Daro inhaled sharply. "It is a challenge."

"Translate," I said quietly.

Daro swallowed. "He asks whether you carry the Fire… or whether you are only smoke."

A test.

I let the words settle into me.

I slowly extended my hand over the water. Closed my eyes. Called gently on the presence that had walked with me since the cavern, since the angel, since the healing of Tyler.

A warmth flared.

Light spiraled through my palm—soft, white, clean.

The water beneath me glowed brighter in response, cascading outward like an answer written across the sea itself.

The warriors jerked back in shock.

The old guardian—the leader of the Western Wind's children—stared up at Nathan with wide, reverent eyes, his spear forgotten in his hand. He sank slowly to one knee, then bowed fully, pressing palms and forehead to the damp earth beside the pool, murmuring fervent words in the ancient, flowing language of his people. The others followed, a ripple of awe spreading through the warriors until half a dozen knelt in a rough semicircle around the water's edge.

Nathan felt the weight of their gaze like a physical thing. His heart twisted. He stepped forward, knelt in the shallow margin of the pool so he was eye-level with the leader, and gently placed a hand on the man's weathered shoulder.

The words came before he even formed them—clear, perfect, in the guardian's own tongue, as though the language had been waiting inside him all along, unlocked by the same quiet presence that had guided him since the cavern, since the angel's visit, since Tyler's healing.

"No, my brother," Nathan said softly, the syllables rolling out smooth and sure. "Do not bow to me. I am only a man, a bearer of the flame, nothing more. Worship the Almighty God alone—the One who shaped the winds you follow, who kindled the first fire, who holds the waters in His hand. He is the Living One. To Him alone belongs the glory."

The guardian's head jerked up. His eyes widened in shock, then filled with sudden tears as he heard his mother's tongue spoken by this stranger from across the world. Recognition flooded his face—not of Nathan as a god, but of the truth carried on Nathan's lips. He pressed a trembling hand to his chest, nodding once, deeply, the bow of one who had been corrected and was grateful.

In that same heartbeat, the water beneath Nathan's outstretched hand—clear, cool, barely ankle-deep—erupted without warning.

Flame burst upward from the surface in a brilliant rush, not consuming the water but dancing upon it, golden-orange and impossibly alive. Twin columns of fire rose on either side of Nathan and the guardian, curving gracefully overhead until they met and intertwined, forming a perfect, soaring arch of living flame. The gate of fire hung there, steady and unquenchable, its light bathing the entire clearing in warm, holy radiance. Heat brushed their faces like a summer breeze, carrying the faint scent of cedar and incense, yet it did not burn.

The warriors gasped, some falling back, others dropping fully prostrate. The leader remained on his knees, staring up at the fiery arch with tears streaming down his cheeks, his spear forgotten on the ground.

Daro's voice came hoarse from behind Nathan. "They... they accept you. And they see the truth."

From deep in the jungle, a long, low horn answered—resonant, ancient, vibrating through the earth and the bones of every man present. The sound rolled outward like a summons, and somewhere far beyond the trees, more horns took up the call, echoing across the valley in a chorus that felt like the land itself was awakening.

The arch of fire burned on, framing Nathan and the guardian beneath its golden curve, a living sign that the Almighty had spoken—and that the way forward was open.

A second boat emerged from the shadowed riverway.

At its bow stood a woman with silver hair braided down her back, skin painted with the symbols of ancient priesthood.

Her eyes—bright, piercing, unmistakably knowing—locked on mine.

She stepped onto the rocks with a grace that defied her age.

"I greet the one who carries the Foreign Fire," she said in perfect, unbroken ancestral tongue.

I blinked. "You… you remember me?"

She smiled faintly.

"No. But my mother did. And her mother before her. We have waited for the Firebearer for seven generations."

The team whispered in awe.

She approached and bowed—not in submission, but in recognition.

The moment hung between them like the last breath before dawn. The fiery arch overhead still danced, its golden flames casting flickering warmth across the pool and the faces of the gathered Western Wind people. No one moved. The air smelled of wet stone, blooming night flowers, and the faint, clean smoke of sacred cedar.

Liora's hand remained over Nathan's, her touch steady but not possessive—more like a bridge than a claim. Her eyes, dark and deep as the jungle beyond, held his without flinching.

"You were foretold to come through shining waters," she said again, her voice soft but carrying the weight of generations. "In the old songs of our clan, the seers spoke of a stranger whose arrival would make the sea itself answer. Not with waves, but with light. When your fire touched the water, and it answered with flame… the island awakened. The ancestors stirred in their sleep. The guardians—the ones who watch from the high places and the deep pools—tested you with silence and with wonder. And you passed."

She paused, letting the words settle like rain on parched earth. Around them, the warriors and elders murmured low prayers, some touching their chests, others tracing small symbols in the air—spirals for wind, circles for eternal return.

Nathan bowed his head slightly in respect, feeling the gravity of her words settle into his bones. "My name is Nathan," he said quietly, the name feeling both ordinary and strangely sacred in this place.

Liora mirrored the bow, then placed her free hand over her heart. "I am Liora, Keeper of the Western Wind Clan." Her voice caught, just a fraction. "Keeper of the breath that brings change, the wind that carries seeds and songs and secrets across the world. And…"

She lifted her hand from his chest and placed it gently over his again, palm to palm, as if sealing something unspoken.

"…I have been waiting for you since before my birth."

The words landed softly, but they rippled outward like the light still glowing in the water. Nathan felt the truth in them—not as romance, but as destiny woven long before either of them drew breath. In the clan's lore, passed down through the women who tended the winds and the waters, a daughter of the line was sometimes marked from the womb: one who would recognize the fire-bearer when he came, one whose own light would help guide the awakening.

Liora's name itself was no accident. In the ancient tongue shared across distant peoples—echoes of Hebrew carried on trade winds and forgotten migrations—"Liora" meant "my light," or "light to me," a name given to those destined to bear illumination in dark times. The seers had seen her coming generations ago: a child born under a sky where the Western Wind whispered promises of renewal, a keeper who would stand at the threshold when the stranger arrived through waters turned to shining flame.

She continued, voice steady now. "My mother dreamed of you before she carried me. She saw a man with fire in his hands, stepping onto our shores when the pool lit like stars fallen to earth. The elders sang of it in the long nights: the one who would call the waters to witness, who would bring the flame that does not consume, but reveals. They said the island—our home, our heart—had slumbered too long, waiting for the sign. When you came, and the water answered… we knew."

She glanced up at the arch of fire, still burning bright and harmless above them. "This is the gate our ancestors spoke of— the bridge between what was hidden and what must now be remembered. You carry the flame, Nathan. But the Western Wind has carried the promise of you to us for centuries."

A low chant rose from the gathered people, soft and rhythmic, like wind moving through leaves. It wasn't worship of Nathan; it was gratitude to the One who had sent him, the Almighty whose hand moved in fire and water alike.

Liora met his eyes once more, a quiet smile touching her lips— the smile of someone who had carried a heavy hope for a lifetime and now saw it fulfilled.

"Welcome home, bearer of the flame," she said. "The clan is yours to walk with, if you will."

Nathan felt the warmth in his chest flare brighter, not his own power, but something far greater—confirmation that every step, every trial, every answered prayer had led precisely here.

The arch of fire pulsed once, as if in agreement, then slowly began to fade, leaving behind only the gentle glow of the pool and the promise of what was to come. The island had awakened. And so had they all.

(14) The Mirror of the Ancients – Reunion and Reckoning

Nathan's POV

Liora gestured with quiet authority. "Come. The tribe must see you."

The warriors escorted us up a winding path carved directly into the mountainside, steps worn smooth by centuries of feet. The air grew sweeter as we ascended, wind carrying the faint sound of chants and rhythmic drums drifting from above.

We emerged into a vast plateau village—terraces of stone huts, woven structures draped in flowering vines, lush hanging gardens spilling over cliffs, and crystalline pools fed by the heart of the island itself. Hundreds of islanders gathered, faces upturned, eyes wide with something between reverence and disbelief.

When they saw me, the chants shifted—ancient words rising like waves, calling the Firebearer home.

Children placed flowers at my feet. Elders touched their foreheads in silent blessing. Young warriors crossed their arms in salute.

The humility of it crushed my chest like gravity. I felt small beneath their gaze, unworthy of the hope shining in their eyes, yet carried forward by the same divine current that had guided me here.

Liora led me to a circular platform of white stone etched with swirling patterns—the same patterns found on the archway.

"This is the Mirror of the Ancients," she said, voice hushed with awe. "A place of belonging. A place of memory."

She traced the spiral with her finger, and the stone responded—lighting up in the same warm glow I had seen beneath the sea.

"It recognizes you," she whispered.

"What does it do?" I asked, feeling the pull in my chest deepen.

Liora stepped back. "You will see."

She began chanting—a low, melodic hymn carried by the villagers.

As the chant rose:

- the spirals brightened
- the air thickened
- the sky dimmed around the stone
- every leaf stilled

I felt a tug in my chest. A connection. A sense of being known—not by the tribe, but by the ancestors. The stone beneath me pulsed—once, twice, three times.

Liora gasped. "It accepts you. The Firebearer has come. The prophecy is alive."

I exhaled, overwhelmed by the weight of destiny resting on me.

Liora bowed deeply. "Welcome, Nathan of Foreign Fire. The Western Wind Clan stands ready. Tell us how we may serve."

The clan welcomed my team into their grand hall—a cavernous dome of white coral and volcanic stone, its ceiling painted with spirals of blue and gold that told stories older than written language. Drums softened to a heartbeat rhythm. Torches dimmed. The air settled into reverent expectation.

Liora stood beside me as Daro raised his staff. The hall's murmurs fell away instantly.

"We have come with news," Daro announced. "News our tribe has carried for generations but never fulfilled—until now."

Liora inclined her head. "Speak. The island listens."

Daro glanced at me. I gave a gentle nod—permission to reveal what few had ever seen.

Eliah unrolled a shimmering sheet of projection cloth. Images formed across it—not drawings, but memory-echoes captured by the tribe's spiritual archivists, from Gabriel's viewpoint and my own direct account.

The hall gasped.

They saw the Bridge—that impossible structure of living stone, pulsing darkness, arrogance carved into physical form. They saw the anomaly beneath it. The armies stirring under the earth. The night it awoke.

Liora held her breath, clutching the edge of her mantle.

Then they saw me—bursting into holy flame, light radiating through armor not forged by human hands, calling down the fire of God with a command that shook the heavens.

They saw the explosion of divine wrath, the collapse of the Bridge, the mountain splitting, the stone dissolving like burning parchment.

"It was destroyed," Daro said softly, "by the hand of God. And by the one foretold—the Foreign Fire."

A ripple of awe passed across the clan. Children pressed closer to their mothers. Warriors knelt without realizing it.

Liora whispered, "Then... the evil our ancestors feared is gone."

I bowed my head. "By God's mercy. Yes."

Talem and Naris carried forward relics wrapped in protective cloths.

"We bring what remains of the old unity," Talem said. "Pieces of history lost when our people scattered."

He opened the first cloth.

A crescent-shaped metal fragment, etched with the symbol of the Four Winds.

Liora inhaled sharply. "Our crest."

Another—a carved stone tablet with spiraling patterns similar to the Mirror beneath our feet.

Another—an ancient bracelet of bone and silver, runes matching the archway I had uncovered.

Liora shivered. "These… these belong to us. They were broken when the tribes fled captivity. You carry the sister pieces."

"We hoped," Talem said softly, "you still carried yours."

Liora motioned. Two elders brought forward a chest of island driftwood. Inside were matching relics—the other halves.

When the pieces were placed beside each other, the runes aligned perfectly—the carvings meeting like reunited family, the shapes clicking together with audible resonance. For a fleeting moment, they glowed.

The hall erupted in awed cheers.

"We remember!" one woman cried. "We belong!" a young warrior shouted.

I felt the joy surge like a wave.

When calm returned, Liora spoke.

"Our ancestors hid on this island not by chance. We fled here during the scattering, guided by the Sea Spirit—what you now call the Holy One. We preserved traditions the mainland forgot. Songs. Runes. Rituals. And…"

Her eyes glimmered.

"…we preserved the door."

Daro stiffened. "The door?"

Liora nodded. "Follow."

She led us along a narrow path that wound upward through thick ferns and ancient banyans until we reached a wide stone overlook perched high above the village. The air here was thinner, sharper, scented with salt and the faint smoke of distant cooking fires. Liora stopped at the edge and pointed downward toward a series of cliffs that framed the far side of the valley.

From this height, the stone looked… wrong. Too perfect. The natural rock had been shaped into sweeping geometric arcs— half-circles, quarter-circles, interlocking like the bones of something enormous buried just beneath the surface. The pattern stirred a deep ache in my chest, the same pull I'd felt when the arch first rose from the earth back in the valley.

Before Liora could speak, the pressure returned—stronger this time. A tug from somewhere deeper than bone, a divine summons that made my skin hum.

"Everyone—stand back," I said, voice tight.

Light erupted from my core—white, blinding, pure. It raced along my arms, my legs, my spine, igniting into holy flame that danced like liquid glass, cool yet alive. The fire didn't burn me; it held me.

Gasps ripped through the group. Liora dropped to her knees, hands clasped, eyes wide with something between terror and recognition.

"It is him," she breathed. "The Firebearer."

I felt the ground release me. My body lifted—slow at first, then steady, guided by an unseen hand. I rose above the treetops, the village shrinking beneath me, the wind rushing past my ears in a soft, reverent sigh.

At the apex, high enough to see the whole island laid out like a map, I closed my eyes and reached across the bond that had grown between us since the beginning.

Gabriel. We found them. The Western Wind Children. And... something else.

His presence answered instantly, warm and alert across the miles.

Show me.

I let the divine fire expand my sight. It stretched outward like wings of light, carrying every detail in perfect clarity. I sent it all to him:

- The cliffs below, shaped into massive, symmetrical arcs that mirrored the hidden structures we'd uncovered beneath the ancient Bridge.
- The stonework—seamless, unweathered, indistinguishable from the constructs that had waited centuries for the right summons.
- The glowing runes etched into the rock, visible only from this angle, pulsing soft blue-white like veins of starlight.
- And then the outline—clear, unmistakable, heart-stopping—of a colossal circular door set into the mountainside, half-concealed by centuries of vine and earth. Its edges were perfectly smooth, its surface

unmarked, as though it had been carved yesterday yet sealed for millennia.

Gabriel's breath caught across the bond, sharp and audible even from halfway around the world.

Nathan... that's an entrance. To something vast. A chamber, a vault, a way through. Whatever it guards, it's been waiting for this.

The vision faded as I willed it. The flames around me softened, dimming to a gentle shimmer. I descended slowly, deliberately, touching down on the overlook once more with the lightness of a leaf settling.

Liora rose to meet me, trembling, tears shining on her cheeks.

"You saw it," she whispered. "The Door of Returning."

I nodded, still feeling the echo of the sight in my bones. "Yes."

Her expression was a storm of emotions—relief, sorrow, fragile hope.

"Then you understand why our people stayed here all these generations."

"Not entirely," I said gently, "but I will learn from you. Whatever this door is, whatever it opens to—I need to know."

Not everyone welcomed the revelation.

A group of warriors stepped forward from the shadows of the path, led by a broad-shouldered man whose presence seemed to carry the weight of the cliffs themselves. His name, I would learn, was Rurik. His jaw was set, eyes hard with the stubborn loyalty of someone who had never known another home.

"We honor your power, Firebearer," Rurik said, voice low and steady. "The flames you carry, the signs you bring—they speak truth. But we do not abandon our ways. The sea raised us. The island fed us. These cliffs protect us. We are not mainlanders. We do not wish to leave."

He planted his spear in the stone with a dull thud, a quiet declaration.

Liora looked at him, then at me, caught between the old promise and the new reality.

The door waited below—silent, patient, immense.

And the choice, it seemed, would not be mine alone.

Murmurs rose—some agreeing, others shaking their heads.

A second group—led by a young woman named Kessa—countered:

"Our ancestors fled, Rurik. They always intended to rejoin the tribe when the foreign tribes fell, and God restored us. The prophecy says we return. You would ignore that?"

Rurik's eyes narrowed.

I lifted my hands.

"Please, we come in peace. I did not come to uproot anyone. Your home is sacred. Yes, the Almighty God is restoring the tribe. There is a new chief rising. A new land is being blessed. A future promised."

Rurik crossed his arms. "We have a future here."

"Yes," I said softly, "but you do not understand the whole of it."

The hall fell silent.

I continued, voice calm but resolute.

"I will not force your path. The choice is yours. Stay in peace… or come in hope. But know this—the world beyond the sea is ever changing. And if you remain hidden forever, the change will reach you anyway. You can face it as a small group, or we can all face it together—united as one massive tribe once again."

Liora bowed her head.

"He speaks truth."

Rurik looked away, jaw clenched.

The debate was far from over.

But the spark had been lit.

(15) Shadows Beneath the Waves

The clan's celebration fires burned late into the night, crackling and popping as embers drifted upward like tiny stars returning home. Laughter and song carried on the warm breeze from the village below, but Nathan could not rest. He sat alone on the edge of the overlook, legs dangling over the drop, the cool stone beneath him grounding him while his mind refused to settle.

Liora's earlier words looped through his thoughts like a persistent echo: "The Sea Spirit guided our ancestors here."

The phrase should have been beautiful—poetic, even. A story of divine guidance across endless waters to a place of refuge. But something inside Nathan recoiled. Not with fear, exactly. Not the cold dread of danger. It was discernment—sharp, instinctive, the kind that had grown in him through years of walking closely with the Holy Spirit.

He knew the feel of *that* presence intimately now. It was warm yet fierce, like sunlight on skin after a long night; comforting yet convicting, gently exposing what needed to change; holy yet intimate, drawing near without overwhelming. The Holy Spirit never demanded worship for Himself—He always pointed to the Father and the Son. He brought clarity, peace that settled the soul, fruit that lasted: love, joy, patience, self-control. When the Spirit moved, there was life, conviction that led to repentance, and a quiet assurance that everything was held securely in God's hands.

But the energy pulsing beneath this island… it was different.

Old. Immeasurably old, like the weight of centuries pressed into the rock itself. Heavy, as if the ground remembered ancient pacts, blood offerings, whispered bargains made under storm-lashed skies. Watching. Not passively observing, but expectant— waiting for something, measuring every breath, every step, every word spoken in its presence. That expectancy carried no warmth. It felt calculating, patient in the way a predator is patient, holding still until the moment is right.

Nathan closed his eyes and tested it the way he'd learned to test every spirit: against the unchanging truth of Scripture, against the character of the God he knew. *Beloved, do not believe every spirit, but test the spirits to see whether they are from God* (1 John 4:1). The Holy Spirit exalted Christ, brought freedom, and bore witness to truth. This… this felt like it waited to *claim*. To bind. To exact a price that had been deferred for generations.

He thought of the Door of Returning hidden in the cliffs—the massive, sealed circle that had waited untouched for so long. Was it truly a door of return, a way back to something holy? Or had the island's guardians—whatever they were—guarded it for their own purposes, using the clan's faithfulness as a living seal?

A chill moved through him, not from the night air but from deeper within. Expectant spirits were rarely pure ones. The Bible was full of warnings about entities that masqueraded as light, that demanded allegiance under the guise of protection, that watched and waited to ensnare. Familiar spirits, deceiving angels of light, powers of darkness that twisted truth just enough to make it palatable.

Nathan exhaled slowly, rubbing his palms together against the sudden cold in his bones. He wasn't here to condemn the people—they had survived, preserved their ways, kept the flame of hope alive in isolation. But he couldn't ignore the distinction. The Holy Spirit had brought him here, not to bow to the island's ancient watchers, but to bring the true Light that exposed every shadow.

He whispered a quiet prayer into the night: "Lord, give me wisdom. Show me what is Yours and what is not. Let Your Spirit lead, not the voices of the deep."

The fires below danced on, oblivious. But Nathan felt the island's expectancy shift—just slightly—like something ancient had heard him and was now listening more closely.

He rose to his feet. Sleep would not come tonight. There was work ahead: listening, testing, discerning. The celebration might continue, but the real battle—the one fought in the unseen—had only just begun.

The clan's celebration fires burned late into the night, crackling high and sending sparks spiraling into the velvet sky like prayers finally released. Laughter and rhythmic drumming drifted up from the village, mingling with the salty breeze off the sea, but Nathan could not rest. He slipped away from the festivities, cloak pulled tight against the cooling air, and returned to the team's large canvas tent glowing softly with lantern light.

Inside, the space felt alive with urgency. Tables groaned under the weight of unearthed treasures: yellowed scrolls tied with frayed cords, fragmented maps stained by centuries of salt and time, hasty sketches of rune-carved stones, and leather-bound journals filled with pictograph script that seemed to shift when stared at too long. Talem, Naris, Kessa, Siyah, and two of the island warriors looked up as Nathan ducked through the flap, their faces etched with the same restless energy he felt.

"We found something," Talem said immediately, voice low and urgent. "Something… large. And it changes everything."

Nathan shed his cloak, letting it drop to the woven mat, and joined them at the central table. The lantern flames danced across their features, casting long shadows that made the room feel smaller, more intimate—and more shadowed.

Naris opened an aged journal with reverent care—pages brittle as dry leaves, ink faded to a ghostly reddish-brown. "This was written by one of the island's first spiritual leaders after the scattering. Right after the tribes fled the mainland."

He laid the journal down gently, revealing a folded parchment pressed between its pages like a hidden heartbeat.

"Read the verse," Naris urged.

Talem cleared his throat, voice steady but thick with the weight of what followed.

"When the tribes fled the Destroyer's shadow, those of the Western Wind hid upon the waters. But the sea they trusted had a hunger of its own."

Nathan stiffened. The words landed like cold water on hot skin.

Talem continued, slower now.

"A spirit unseen walked among them—not the Spirit of Heaven, but an ancient echo of the deep. It comforted them in exile but demanded silence in return. It promised protection, but bound them to its depths. It fed on their offerings, their isolation, their fear of returning."

A chill crawled up Nathan's spine, familiar and piercing—the same discernment he'd felt since setting foot on this ground.

Naris spoke quietly, eyes on the page. "The Western Wind Children believed this spirit was their protector. A guardian born of the sea, kind in the storm. But this prophecy… it suggests otherwise. It calls it a counterfeit. A watcher that mimics light but thrives in silence and shadow."

Nathan felt the confirmation settle into his chest like a stone dropped into still water—ripples spreading outward. "It's not God," he said, voice low but certain. "It never was. The Holy Spirit points to Christ, convicts with love, and brings freedom. This… this demands loyalty through fear and isolation. It's a pretender."

Siyah nodded, her voice trembling slightly. "When we first stepped foot on the island, I felt a vibration under the earth. Not holy. Not neutral. Something stirring. Something claiming territory—like it's been waiting, measuring us."

Nathan pressed his palms together, lifting his eyes to the tent's canvas ceiling as if searching for stars through the fabric. "Then this island is occupied—spiritually. Not by the sea itself, but by something that's made the sea its stronghold. Something that's kept the door sealed, kept your people cut off."

"And the door?" Talem asked, leaning forward. "Does it… lead to it? To this thing?"

Nathan shook his head slowly. "No. The door predates the spirit. It wasn't created by whatever resides under the island. It's older—tied to the original call of the remnant, the promise of return and restoration. But whatever that thing is… it doesn't want the door opened. It's afraid of what comes through."

Silence settled like dust after a storm—thick, heavy, expectant.

Naris pulled another scroll from the pile—ancient, brittle, its wax seal cracked but intact until now. "We found this too. Liora didn't know it existed. It must have been hidden until the right moment—until now."

Nathan broke the seal carefully. The text inside was written in spiraling script, unmistakably tribal but laced with warnings that read like a cry across centuries.

He began to read aloud, voice steady despite the growing chill in the air:

"When the Firebearer comes, the island shall shake with remembrance. The old guardian will awaken in jealousy, for its time will be at an end. It has fed on silence and fear, twisting the sea's voice into its own. The Children of the Western Wind shall face a choice: return to the One True God, who parted the waters and crushed the chaos in the deep, or remain bound to the sea that hides the Shadow."

Nathan's blood chilled. The words echoed the ancient biblical imagery—Rahab, Leviathan, the sea monsters God had defeated at creation, symbols of chaos and rebellion crushed under His sovereign hand.

Talem finished the passage with a breathless whisper: "This prophecy… it anticipates you."

And something else.

A battle.

Not with men. Not with clans. But with the unseen—with powers that had masqueraded as protectors, demanding silence while feeding on devotion meant for the Almighty alone.

Nathan pressed his fingers to the page, sensing the truth resonate through him as a tuning fork struck in the deep. "Then I need to call on Heaven," he said softly. "Because something dark is about to be unmasked. And it knows we're coming for the door."

Earlier that day, on the cliff's edge, Nathan had lifted his eyes to the patterned cliffs and felt that divine tug again. Instinctively, he had reached out to the drone operator through the telepathic channel he and Gabriel had been strengthening.

Spread the drones. Measure everything. Show me what I can't see from here.

Now the results were displayed across a stretched canvas in the tent—high-resolution images, thermal heat signatures, density scans, topographical gradients glowing in soft blues and reds.

Kessa pointed to the overlay. "The door you saw from above? It's real. And it's massive—easily thirty meters across, sealed with precision we can't replicate even today."

Siyah added, voice hushed, "It's sealed from the inside. And something behind it… isn't natural. The scans show an energy signature—low, rhythmic, almost like a heartbeat beneath stone. It's been dormant, but it's stirring now."

Nathan absorbed every frame: the curve of the arch, the glowing runes pulsing in patterns that mirrored the ancient Bridge constructs, the faint outline of the circular door hidden under centuries of vine and earth.

"Whatever's down there," he murmured, "wants to stay hidden. It's been guarding its territory, using the clan's isolation as its cage."

The warriors exchanged uneasy glances, hands tightening on spear shafts.

Talem whispered, "Nathan… why would the sea spirit hide the door?"

Nathan set his jaw. "Because it isn't a sea spirit. It's a counterfeit. A pretender that's twisted their faith, demanded silence instead of worship, and offered comfort in exchange for bondage. And the door is a threat to it—a way back to the true God, to the remnant, to freedom."

The next morning, the council fire roared high inside the great coral dome, flames leaping like witnesses to the moment. The clan elders sat in a semicircle on woven mats, ceremonial white clay streaked across their faces in traditional lines of protection and mourning. Liora sat among them, hands clasped tightly in her lap, eyes bright with anticipation…and a flicker of dread.

Nathan stepped forward, relics in hand, the forgotten prophecy scroll tucked under his arm as a sword sheathed but ready.

"I have learned more about your history," he said, voice carrying clearly over the crackle of the fire. "And it is not what you were taught."

The hall stilled instantly. Even the flames seemed to lean in.

Nathan laid the relics gently before the elders—the journal, the hidden scroll, fragments of maps that showed the door's outline. "These pieces were broken when your ancestors fled. They are reunited now because God is calling your tribe back into wholeness. Back into truth."

A ripple spread through the room—murmurs, sharp intakes of breath. Even Rurik, the defiant one, leaned forward, eyes narrowed.

Nathan unrolled the ancient prophecy, its spiraling script catching the firelight like living ink.

"Your people were deceived," he said softly. "Not by evil men. Not by the Holy Spirit. But by something ancient… something of the deep. A spirit that offered comfort in exile but demanded silence in return. It promised protection but fed on your isolation. It twisted the sea's voice into its own, keeping you from the One who truly parted the waters and crushed the chaos beneath."

Murmurs rose again—uneasy, trembling, some hands reaching instinctively for protective charms.

Nathan continued, revealing the deception of the "sea spirit," the warnings of jealousy and awakening, the call back to the true God who had already defeated every pretender in the deep.

The hall grew tense, breaths held in cautious, trembling silence.

Nathan finished reading, lowered the scroll, and looked to the elders.

"What I speak is truth," he said gently but firmly. "But truth must be received, not forced."

A long pause stretched, heavy as the sea itself.

Then Liora spoke.

Her voice was quiet at first, unsure if it would carry—but the chamber's acoustics embraced her words like a cradle.

"Tell us," she whispered, "what Heaven has shown you."

Her request fell over the council like sacred wind. Tears shimmered in her eyes, unhidden.

She felt her breath catch.

The Firebearer. Standing before us.

She had known the moment she saw him glowing in holy fire on the cliffs. Her soul had bowed before her body did. Her mother had whispered stories of this moment when she was a child: "The Firebearer will come when our exile has ended. His presence will expose what is true and what is false."

Now the truth was landing like lightning in her chest.

"The Spirit of the Seas is not God."

The words struck deeper than any spear. If Nathan spoke truth—and her spirit knew he did—then every prayer they had whispered to the sea, every offering cast into the waves, every storm interpreted as guidance… had been misaligned. Not evil. Not rebellious. Just misdirected.

Forgive us… We didn't know.

She looked at Nathan again—really looked. There was no judgment in him. Only sorrow. Only compassion burning like sunrise.

When she whispered, "Tell us what Heaven has shown you," it wasn't skepticism.

It was a plea.

Show me the God my ancestors lost.

Show me how to return.

Show me how to make this right.

Tears slid down her face, warm and unhidden.

For the first time in her life—she felt the true Holy Spirit moving in the room, gentle yet undeniable, convicting without crushing, drawing without demanding.

And she prayed silently, fiercely: *Lead us home, Firebeurer. Lead us home.*

Nathan continued, voice steady.

"I will not force your path. But know this: a false spirit has claimed this island for millennia. It will not tolerate the truth. And if you remain bound to it, your peace will not last. God is calling you home—to join the restored tribe. To join your people. To walk out from under the shadow and into the light that never demands silence."

The elders exchanged stunned glances.

One elder whispered, "Is this true, Liora?"

Liora rose slowly, her cheeks wet, her voice trembling but resolute.

"Yes. I believe him. And… I believe we have been mistaken. Our ancestors trusted something that felt like guidance but was not of God. The Firebearer's light exposes it. We must listen."

Gasps rippled through the dome.

Some were in awe.

Some were fearful.

Some were in resistance.

The council fire roared high inside the great coral dome, flames leaping like living witnesses, casting jagged shadows across the curved walls etched with generations of ancestral spirals. Smoke curled upward, thick with the scent of sandalwood and dried kelp, stinging eyes and throats alike. The elders sat in their semicircle on woven pandanus mats, white ceremonial clay streaked across their faces in lines of protection, mourning, and resolve—marks that now seemed to waver in the firelight. Liora remained seated among them, hands clasped so tightly her knuckles paled, her dark eyes fixed on Nathan with a mix of fierce hope and quiet terror.

Rurik shot to his feet, broad shoulders filling the space, his spear still planted in the packed earth like an accusation. The muscles in his jaw bunched, corded with the strain of holding back years of inherited duty.

"You would abandon our protector?" His voice boomed, raw and resonant, echoing off the dome like thunder trapped underwater. "You would betray the traditions that kept us alive when the mainland burned? The sea gave us breath when we had none. The cliffs sheltered us. And now you call it a lie?"

The words hung heavy, charged. Several younger warriors shifted, hands drifting toward weapons, their loyalty to Rurik—a man who had led fishing crews through typhoons and buried brothers lost to the deep—tugging at them visibly.

Liora rose slowly, her movements deliberate, the hem of her woven robe brushing the floor. When she spoke, her voice carried unexpected strength, tempered steel beneath the tremor.

"We are not betraying tradition," she said, each word measured, as if carved from the same coral as the dome. "We are correcting its course. We are returning to the True One who has always been waiting—before the sea whispered, before the cliffs rose, before our ancestors ever set foot on these waters. The stories we were told were half-told. The comfort we felt was borrowed. And I… I will not pass that half-truth to my children."

Her gaze swept the council, lingering on the elders who had taught her the old chants, then returning to Rurik. Tears gleamed, but did not fall. "We survived. But survival is not the same as thriving. We were kept, not blessed."

Nathan stepped between them, hands open at his sides—palms up, empty, a gesture of peace rather than power. The firelight played across his face, highlighting the faint scars from earlier trials, the steady calm in his eyes that came from having walked through literal flame and not been consumed.

"You each have a choice," he said, voice low but carrying the quiet authority of someone who had heard Heaven speak and obeyed. "I honor that. God does not force hearts—He invites them. But restoration always reveals the shadows that hid in the light. Those shadows must be removed before a holy and just God."

He paused, letting the words settle, then met Rurik's glare directly.

"Whatever your choice, I am being directed to face this threat. The door will open. The truth will come through. Do you hold enough confidence in this 'thing'—this ancient watcher that demands silence and feeds on fear—that you will stand against the presence of God's message to you now? Or will you let Him speak?"

The challenge hung there, not as an ultimatum, but as an open door. The dome seemed to contract around them; the fire snapped once, sharply, as if the island itself had drawn a breath.

Silence fell, thick as ocean fog rolling in from the night sea. No one moved. The elders' painted faces were unreadable, caught between generations of memory and the sudden, sharp pull of something new. The younger warriors looked to Rurik, then to Liora, then to Nathan—torn between the protector they knew and the unknown promise standing before them.

The council had heard the truth.

The island, as if listening, seemed to hold its breath. The distant crash of waves against the cliffs grew muffled, subdued, as though the sea itself waited for the next word.

And deep beneath the cliffs—something old, something jealous, something awakened and long-accustomed to dominion— shifted in the dark. Stone groaned faintly, almost imperceptibly, a low vibration felt more in the bones than the ears. Its expectancy had turned to hunger, a cold, patient appetite that had waited centuries for challengers and now sensed one who carried real fire.

(16) The Deep That Hungers

The council had barely adjourned—elders rising stiffly from pandanus mats, voices fracturing into stunned murmurs—when the island replied.

A tremor rolled up through the coral dome, not seismic chaos but deliberate, sentient pressure: the earth inhaling once, slow and deep, as though tasting the words still hanging in the smoke-thick air. Stone groaned faintly beneath their feet. Lanterns swayed on their chains; shadows stretched and snapped back like whips.

Liora's palm slapped against her sternum, fingers splaying wide. "The island… it hasn't moved like this since the great typhoon of my grandmother's youth."

Nathan felt the vibration climb his spine like cold mercury. This was no tectonic indifference. This was a response—personal, wounded, furious. The false guardian had heard every syllable of truth spoken in the dome and now answered in the only language it knew: dominion.

Outside, the night sea turned savage. Waves that had lapped gently moments earlier reared black and glassy, twice the height of men, and smashed the cliffs with artillery force. Each impact boomed low and guttural, the sound burrowing into ribcages, rattling teeth. Spray exploded inland, carrying a dark, oily shimmer—not the clean iridescence of holy fire, but a counterfeit gleam, thick as spilled ink, clinging to skin and stone like accusation made visible.

Warriors poured from the hall, spears glinting in torchlight, shouting half-formed orders as they sprinted toward the shoreline. Mothers snatched children from the paths; dogs bolted, tails low, howling in primal panic. The air tasted of salt, wet rot, and something older—coppery, like blood long dried on ancient altars.

Beneath the surface, the sea began to glow. Not plankton's soft bioluminescence, but a sickly blue-green luminescence spiraling in thick, deliberate veins, coiling and uncoiling like capillaries feeding something vast and awake. The patterns pulsed in rhythm—slow, predatory, measuring.

Liora whispered, voice cracking like dry coral, "It wakes."

Talem's throat worked. "The prophecy… 'the old guardian will awaken in jealousy.'"

Nathan's stomach clenched. The spiritual atmosphere had thickened; pressure pressed against his eardrums, his temples, the soft hollow beneath his sternum. The air itself tasted metallic, fouled with the scent of old bargains, salt-crusted offerings, and the faint, nauseating sweetness of fear long fermented.

A rogue wave reared, monstrous, black-rimmed, and struck the coast with cataclysmic force. The ground jumped. Mist billowed inland, dark and glittering, settling on faces and arms like a second skin of dread.

Warriors recoiled, spears lifted uselessly toward the unseen. The water sucked back with a roar, exposing glistening black rock—and then it spoke.

Not with language. With pressure.

A single, bone-deep pulse rolled up from the ocean floor—slow, deliberate, a spiritual shockwave that washed across the island like psychic tide. Children screamed. Livestock thrashed in pens. Torches along the paths guttered, flared sickly green, then died again. The wind reversed direction, cold and wet and wrong, pressing against Nathan's face like the clammy palm of something possessive, jealous, ancient.

The cliffs trembled. Palm fronds hissed in sudden, hostile gusts. Shadows writhed across the sand though the moon remained unveiled.

The Door of Returning—still veiled in stone and vine—began to hum.

Not in the invitation. In protest.

The hum deepened to a groan, the groan to a rumble, the rumble to a roar that rolled up through the earth like the growl of a beast roused after centuries of feigned sleep.

Liora dropped to her knees, palms pressing into the dirt, voice breaking. "It knows you've come to break its hold."

Nathan stepped forward, boots grinding coral gravel. He lifted one hand, palm outward—not surrender, but unyielding defiance.

"No," he said, voice cutting clean through the gale. "I've come to reveal the truth. It reacts because truth will expose it—and it cannot survive exposure."

Behind him, warriors of both sides gathered—those loyal to generations of sea-worship, those already half-converted by the light they had glimpsed—faces pale, eyes wide, fear welding them together where doctrine had divided.

The wind shifted again: colder, wetter, heavier. It settled on Nathan's skin like the touch of a jealous hand—clammy, insistent, territorial.

Gabriel's voice sliced through the bond, sharp with alarm. *Nathan—what's happening?*

The island is waking up. Not in a good way. I need Heaven at my back.

I'm with you.

Gabriel's presence locked in beside him—distant yet immovable, an anchor across oceans.

But this battle belonged to Nathan alone.

He walked to the cliff's edge where the waves now churned like boiling tar. The sea hissed—yes, hissed, a living, venomous sound.

"Enough!" Nathan shouted, voice cracking like lightning across the water.

The sea answered with another towering black wave.

Nathan drew a single, deep breath.

And called.

He raised one arm high, fingers spread toward the sky.

"God of Heaven," he declared, breath igniting with holy fire, "Your people call for help. Let Your host descend."

Time arrested.

Wind froze mid-surge. Waves hung suspended, mid-crash. The air pulled inward in a violent, collective inhale—as though creation itself braced for impact.

Then—

The sky tore open.

Light lanced downward in a blinding column, shredding clouds with the sound of a thousand thunderclaps layered into one apocalyptic chord. The brilliance was so fierce it burned retinas, yet no one could look away.

Figures plunged from the radiance—not drifting, not floating, but descending like shock troops deployed into contested territory.

Armor gleamed like molten stars. Swords burned white-hot. Wings unfurled in blinding sheets of radiance that scorched the night.

The first angel struck the ground— BOOM —the earth split.

Another— BOOM —the cliffs fractured in lightning veins.

Then the full legion— BOOM-BOOM-BOOM —the mountains themselves shook. Dust billowed outward in choking clouds. Palm trees bowed as if in worship or terror. The sea screamed—a high, piercing wail of rage and despair.

Liora fell face-down, arms outstretched in raw awe and fear.

Half the tribe collapsed.

Even the warriors trembled, spears slipping from sweat-slick palms.

Nathan felt the shockwave race up his spine—and something inside answered.

A divine surge. The archangels encircled him once more, as they had in the earliest days of his calling.

A mantle descended—living, breathing, real.

The armor of God manifested upon his body, not as metaphor but as radiant substance:

- The Breastplate of Righteousness blazed across his chest like white fire
- The Belt of Truth buckled around his waist, runes pulsing with unshakeable certainty
- The Shield of Faith formed on his left arm with the force of a newborn star
- The Helmet of Salvation snapped over his head in a ring of golden light

- The Boots of the Gospel of Peace slammed into the sand with sacred shock, anchoring him immovably
- And finally…

The sword.

A blade descended from the column of light—forged from scripture itself, edge lined with living verses burning in holy flame.

When Nathan grasped the hilt, it roared with power that shook the air and silenced the wind.

"Good God…" one warrior breathed, voice cracking.

Liora sobbed openly.

Even Rurik dropped to his knees, face ashen.

Nathan raised the sword high.

The angels behind him straightened, saluting in perfect formation.

Heaven waited.

Beneath the cliff, the great circular doorway ignited in violent protest.

Symbols flared in frantic spirals. Edges burned with unnatural blue fire. The rock screamed.

Talem shouted over the chaos, "Nathan! The drones—something's behind the door—something huge!"

Nathan and the heavenly host advanced, holding perfect poise before the sealed stone. He pointed the sword.

Scripture erupted from the blade like lightning strikes across the surface:

"The LORD will go forth like a warrior; He shall stir up zeal like a man of war! He will shout, indeed, and He will raise a war cry. He will prevail against His enemies." — Isaiah 42:13

"For nothing is hidden except to be made manifest; nor is anything secret except to come to light." — Mark 4:22

"Nothing is covered up that will not be revealed, or hidden that will not be known." — Luke 12:2 & Luke 8:17

"So have no fear of them, for nothing is covered that will not be revealed, or hidden that will not be known." — Matthew 10:26

"Though his hatred be covered with deception, his wickedness will be exposed in the assembly." — Proverbs 26:26

The door detonated.

Stone exploded outward—not as dust or rubble, but as shimmering particles of holy light, the ancient barrier shredded to reveal the pit beyond.

A blinding white beam shot downward from heaven, piercing straight into the exposed darkness.

The sea spirit shrieked—a sound between the death-cry of a leviathan and the wail of a demon being cast out.

The island bucked violently. Trees uprooted. Rocks cascaded. The coastline heaved.

A vast shape writhed in the pit—not water, not flesh, not shadow—but a spiritual entity coiled like the serpent of the deep. Its form flickered, unstable—monstrous one heartbeat, mist the next—desperately seeking a shape it could no longer sustain.

The heavenly beam scorched it. It shrieked again, thrashing in agony.

Nathan stepped into the mouth of the pit, armor blazing, sword raised.

"You deceived these people," he declared, voice layered with divine resonance that drowned the chaos. "You disguised yourself as comfort. As guidance. As a protector. But the truth has come—and truth is your undoing."

The spirit recoiled, hissing, coiling tighter in futile defiance.

Nathan lifted the sword higher.

The angels fell into formation behind him—a radiant, terrifying phalanx of divine authority.

"By the authority of the Almighty God," Nathan commanded, voice thundering across sea and stone, "and in the mighty name of Jesus Christ, the Messiah, you will release this land. You will release His people. You will release every heart you bound in lies and silence."

Heaven answered.

Fire roared down the angelic ranks—pure, holy flame that consumed only deception, leaving flesh and stone untouched.

The spirit shrieked, blinded by the white beam. It lunged once—desperate, furious—then recoiled as Nathan advanced.

He spoke the final, decisive strike, voice ringing like a bell across creation:

"The light shines in the darkness, and the darkness has not overcome it!" — John 1:5

The blade descended.

Heaven descended with it.

A shockwave tore through the pit—pure light exploding outward in every direction.

The sea spirit was obliterated in a final, deafening roar of divine fire.

The water outside the cliffs crashed back into natural rhythm. The wind gentled to a soft, cleansing breath. The trembling ceased.

Silence fell—clean, deep, holy.

Then—a single, exhaled breath from Nathan:

"Thank You… God."

The angels bowed their heads in silent salute.

The tribe began to weep—not in fear, but in release, in awe, in gratitude so profound it hurt.

For the first time in millennia, the island was free.

The false guardian was gone.

The true King had returned.

(17) A Land Made New

The silence after the spirit's destruction was unlike any Nathan had ever known—deeper even than the hush that had fallen in the caverns back home after the first angel appeared. It was not merely the absence of sound. It was the presence of peace so thick it pressed against the lungs, sweet and heavy, like breathing after being underwater for years.

The ocean, moments before a roaring beast intent on swallowing the cliffs, now sighed like a child finally asleep after fever dreams. Waves lapped at the shore in soft, apologetic strokes, each one carrying away centuries of dread, salt, and shadowed offerings. The water itself seemed lighter, clearer, as though a film of spiritual grime had been rinsed away.

The air changed. Not gradually, but all at once—like a window thrown open in a room sealed for generations. It tasted clean, alive, carrying the scent of wet stone, night-blooming jasmine, and something indefinable: the fragrance of grace after long exile.

Warriors stood frozen, spears hanging limp in their hands, staring at one another as though seeing strangers for the first time. Faces streaked with soot and tears reflected the dying glow of the holy fire. Liora staggered backward a step, palm pressed hard over her heart, breath coming in shallow, astonished gasps.

Even the palm trees seemed to straighten, their fronds rustling in a breeze no longer choked by oppression, whispering now in quiet wonder instead of fear.

Nathan remained at the cliff's edge, the radiant armor of God slowly dimming to a gentle, living luminescence—like dawn light caught in crystal. The angels behind him held formation only a heartbeat longer, wings half-furled, swords lowered in salute. One by one, they bowed their heads toward the trembling tribe—not in condescension, but in reverence for the courage it had taken to choose truth over comfort.

Then, with a soft folding of brilliance, a quiet folding of wings, they ascended. Light rippled upward in gentle waves, sweeping across the island like a final benediction. The land exhaled. And for the first time in centuries, it was free.

Nathan's knees buckled—not from exhaustion, not from the overwhelming awe of celestial warriors, but from the sheer weight of thankfulness that flooded him. He dropped to both knees, forehead pressing into the warm, scarred stone.

"All honor… all glory belongs to You, God," he whispered, voice cracking with emotion. "*You* freed *Your* people. *You* exposed the lie. *You* restored what was broken for so long. Let my life be nothing—nothing—but a witness to *Your* power, *Your* mercy, *Your* relentless love."

The armor dimmed respectfully at his words, as though heaven itself honored the posture of a heart laid bare.

Slowly, he rose. He bent and gathered broken fragments of the shattered doorway—jagged picccs the false spirit had once used to seal away truth. With deliberate care he stacked them, one upon another, forming a simple cairn. Not an altar of sacrifice. A monument of testimony. Like the stones the Hebrews once raised in the wilderness—silent witnesses for generations yet unborn.

When the last stone settled into place, Nathan laid both hands upon the pile, eyes closed. "Let this stand," he murmured, "as a memorial of what You have done here tonight."

A quiet fire—pure, holy, weightless—flowed from his palms. The stones heated, glowed soft gold, and fused together in a single seamless monument. Not to Nathan. Never to Nathan. To God alone.

Behind him, the tribe watched in stunned silence. They had witnessed angels descending in battle array, a false god unmasked and destroyed, light tearing through centuries of darkness—but this simple, humble act of remembrance broke them open. Not in fear. In reverence so deep it hurt.

One by one they fell to their knees—men, women, children, warriors, elders. Some pressed palms to hearts. Some lifted tear-streaked faces to the stars. Some wept openly, shoulders shaking with the release of a bondage they had never fully named.

Together, in ragged, beautiful chorus, they thanked God—for His provision through isolation, His care in the storm, His protection in the shadows, His truth that finally cut through the lie, His rescue that came when hope had almost died.

When the last whispered "Amen" drifted into the night, a reverent cheer rose—not wild, not chaotic, but full and deep, like the single heartbeat of a tribe being reborn.

And it was in this holy quiet after the praise that Liora finally rose. She approached Nathan slowly, knees trembling, eyes shining with unshed tears and fierce joy.

"Firebearer..." she whispered, voice thick. "We have never known this air. Not in my lifetime. Not in my mother's. Not in her mother's. It feels... like breathing for the first time."

Warriors dropped to one knee—not in worship, but in profound reverence. Children clung to one another, wide-eyed and smiling through tears. Elders lifted trembling hands toward heaven.

Rurik approached last. He bowed deeply—deeper than anyone had expected from the proud guardian of tradition—and spoke in a low, raw voice: "We did not know we were enslaved until you broke the chains. Forgive us."

Nathan rested a hand on the man's broad shoulder, voice gentle. "Then you were never unwilling prisoners. Only a people waiting—waiting—for truth to find you."

Liora nodded fiercely, tears spilling freely now. "We return," she declared, voice ringing with sudden certainty. "We return to God. To the greater tribe. To our destiny."

A cheer erupted across the cliffside—joyful, unbroken, rolling out over the newly calmed sea like a wave of its own.

Nathan turned toward the now-ruined doorway. The stone no longer resisted. A faint, sweet breeze drifted from within, carrying the scent of ancient parchment, untouched earth, cedar oil, and something deeper: holiness resting where deception once ruled.

Liora and Talem followed close behind.

"Do you feel that?" Talem asked softly, voice hushed with wonder.

Nathan nodded, throat tight. "Holiness. The Spirit of God settling where darkness once held court."

They descended carefully down the spiral of carved steps now revealed by the broken seal. Torches flared to life the moment Nathan crossed the threshold—flames burning clean white, without smoke or flicker.

The chamber opened wide before them—a vast, circular room buried beneath the cliffs, untouched for centuries, air still and cool and sacred.

And it was not empty.

Talem gasped. "My God…"

Across the chamber:

- Stone tables laden with preserved scrolls, bindings intact, ink still dark
- Relics gleaming softly—bronze vessels, carved ivory, jade seals
- Ancient water jars, sealed with wax that had not cracked
- Symbols of the Four Winds etched in pristine precision along the walls
- And dominating the far wall—a mural stretching the entire length of the chamber, colors vivid as the day they were painted

Nathan walked toward it slowly, heart pounding.

The mural told the story in sweeping, heartbreaking detail:

- The scattering of the tribes under the Destroyer's shadow
- The Western Wind Children fleeing across storm-tossed seas
- Their arrival on this hidden island
- The gradual rise of the false sea spirit, seductive and subtle, twisting comfort into chains
- And at the center, radiant and unmistakable: A figure engulfed in white flame, sword of light raised, standing on the very cliff where Nathan had stood moments ago.

Liora's hand flew to her mouth. "This… is you."

Nathan stared, stunned, the weight of prophecy settling over him like a mantle he had not asked for.

"It was foretold," an elder whispered behind them, voice trembling. "Not only that you would free us… but that your coming would open the way to…"

She could not finish.

Because beneath the painted Firebearer, six spiraling lines extended outward like spokes of a sacred wheel. Each pointed to a carved emblem: North Wind. South Wind. East Wind. West Wind. The Great Center. And the Lost Children.

Talem's whisper was almost reverent. "This is… a map."

On a central pedestal lay a scroll wrapped in gold-thread binding. When Nathan lifted it, his sword—still in hand—flared faintly, recognizing the sacred script.

He unrolled it. The prophecy read, words burning into his spirit:

"When the Foreign Fire frees the Western Wind, the tribes shall rise from hiding. The scattered shall gather. The Lost shall be found. And the path to the Great Center will be revealed."

A chill moved through him. The Great Center. The place of origin. The heart of the tribe before the scattering, before the world broke apart.

Gabriel's voice brushed his mind, gentle yet urgent: *Nathan… are you reading prophecy?*

Yes.

Does it tell us where to go next?

Nathan read the final verse aloud, voice hushed:

"Seek next the Eastward Flame, hidden in the land of storms. For there you will find the child with the Keeper's Mark."

He exhaled, the weight of adventure yet to come settling over him like dawn light. "Yes, Gabriel," he whispered aloud. "It does."

He stepped back out of the chamber into the fresh, newly freed island air. The tribe had gathered, faces alight with hope, waiting, believing.

Liora bowed her head. "What does Heaven ask of us now?"

Nathan held the scroll tightly, feeling its warmth against his palm. "There is another tribe," he said, voice steady and full of promise. "To the east. Hidden in storms. A child waits there—one marked by your ancestors, one who must be found."

Gabriel's voice came again, soft, steady: *We'll prepare for travel. Tyler wants to help. He says… he feels something important happening.*

Nathan smiled faintly, the thought of his son warming him. "Good," he murmured. "He'll need to."

The Western Wind tribe gathered around him as he raised the scroll toward the sky.

"Your freedom is the beginning," Nathan said, voice ringing with quiet certainty. "Now comes the gathering."

The wind shifted—warm, holy, carrying the scent of new dawn.

And the next chapter of destiny began.

(18) The Child of the Keeper's Mark

Tyler & Nathan POV

Tyler woke before dawn—breath sharp in his throat, heart hammering against ribs as though it had been waiting for the moment to break free. The estate bedroom was still dark, curtains heavy with night, but inside him everything was wide open, spirit stretched taut like a sail catching sudden wind, a door flung wide by an unseen hand.

He sat up fast, sheets tangling around his legs, cold sweat prickling across his brow and down his spine. The air felt charged, electric, as if the room itself had held its breath with him.

"Nathan…" he whispered instinctively, the name slipping out before thought, though his dad was an ocean and half a continent away.

Then the vision crashed over him fully—vivid, overwhelming, alive in every detail.

A storm-pierced coastline, black waves exploding against razor rocks, foam whipped into white fury by wind that howled like grief. A stone arch, ancient and weathered, half-buried in wet sand, its curve etched with symbols that pulsed faintly under lightning flashes. A child—no older than Tyler himself— standing barefoot in the gale, clothes plastered to his skin, arm outstretched as though reaching for something only he could see. On his forearm: the symbol. A swirling flame, bright and living, encircled in gold that shimmered against the storm's darkness. The Keeper's Mark.

And a voice—not thunderous, not distant, but intimate, warm, closer than his own heartbeat—spoke one word: "Go."

Tyler gasped, fingers clamping around the bedframe until wood creaked. He knew instantly, bone-deep, soul-deep: He was being summoned. He was being included. He couldn't wait another heartbeat.

He tore from the bed, bare feet slapping cold marble as he ran through the sleeping halls, knocking urgently on Gabriel's door—once, twice, three times.

"Dad—wake up! I saw something. I saw where we have to go!"

Gabriel was up in an instant, door swinging open, already reaching for the tactical pack he kept by the wall. His eyes— sharp, steady—locked on Tyler's face and saw the same fire he'd once watched burn in Nathan's younger days.

"What happened? What did you see?"

Tyler struggled for words; all he had was urgency blazing in his chest like a second heartbeat.

"I need to go to him," he said, voice shaking with certainty. "I need to go to Papa Nathan."

Gabriel searched his son's eyes for only a second, saw the unshakeable resolve there, and nodded once.

"Then we go."

Minutes later, Gabriel's aircraft tore into the pre-dawn sky, engines roaring as they climbed. Tyler sat strapped in beside him, fingers pressed to the window, replaying the vision in relentless loops—the storm, the arch, the mark, the voice. His heart raced with something fiercer than fear: purpose.

The flight stretched long and tense—Gabriel holding the controls steady, glancing at Tyler every few minutes with quiet pride. Tyler traced invisible patterns on his own forearm where the mark had glowed in the dream, feeling the echo of it still tingling beneath his skin.

As they descended toward the Western Wind Island, the tribe below erupted in wonder. Faces turned skyward, hands shielding eyes against the sun. When Tyler climbed out beside Gabriel— taller now, shoulders broadening, carrying the same quiet, unmistakable light—the whispers spread like warm currents through the crowd.

"Firebearer's son..." "He carries the same light..." "No— look—Gabriel's son. The heir..." "Is this the next chief?"

The words followed him, soft and reverent, wrapping around him like a mantle he had not yet asked for.

Nathan pushed through the throng—face breaking into relief so raw it hurt, pride so fierce it shone in his eyes.

"Tyler?"

Tyler didn't wait. He rushed forward, arms wrapping around Nathan, burying his face in his father's chest like he was eight again, the familiar scent of salt and sacred smoke grounding him instantly.

Nathan held him tightly, one hand cradling the back of his son's head, the other steady across his shoulders.

"Hey… hey. I'm here. You're okay."

Gabriel placed a hand on Nathan's shoulder, voice low. "He had a vision."

Nathan eased back just enough to look down at Tyler. "What did you see, sweetheart?"

"A child," Tyler whispered against Nathan's shirt. "He had a mark. A flame inside a circle. And a storm… Papa Nathan, he was waiting… for us."

Nathan exhaled slowly, the words settling like stones in deep water. The Keeper's Mark. The next tribe. The next step.

For the next three hours, Gabriel piloted flight after flight—carrying elders with their wisdom etched in lined faces, families clutching children and memories, tools worn smooth by generations, livestock lowing in nervous protest, sacred items wrapped in soft cloth, scrolls bound in faded leather, relics that still hummed with faint power, and every ounce of the tribe's hope. Other pilots joined, vessels and aircraft shuttling between island and the new tribal center in a steady, determined rhythm.

The people sang as they packed—soft hymns of deliverance, melodies they hadn't dared utter aloud for generations, voices cracking with joy and disbelief. Even Rurik helped, shoulders set with new purpose, hands steady as he loaded crates. Even the skeptics wept openly, tears mixing with laughter.

Freedom had given them courage.

Nathan and Tyler stood on the beach while loading continued, the sun climbing higher, warming the sand beneath their feet. A sudden hush fell over the crowd.

A lone figure approached from the far side of the sand—tall, haggard, eyes burning with desperate, dangerous intelligence. His clothing was a patchwork of tribal markings and scavenged armor—a remnant of the scattering, twisted by years of bitterness into something sharp-edged and wrong.

Nathan recognized it immediately: someone shaped by exile but claimed by resentment.

Tyler's hand tightened around Nathan's sleeve.

The man stopped ten feet away. "You," he hissed. "Foreign Fire."

Nathan stepped protectively in front of Tyler. "I am here to restore the tribes. Not fight our own."

"You restored them," the man spat, pointing at the islanders. "Where was your God when the rest of us were hunted? Scattered? Starving? Where was He when we begged for deliverance and got none?"

Nathan shook his head softly. "He was calling you home. You didn't hear Him."

"I heard something," the man growled. "And it wasn't your God."

Nathan felt Tyler tense beside him. The descendant's aura crackled—not with spiritual power, but with years of anger hardened into cruelty.

"What do you want?" Nathan asked gently.

"You freed the island," the man said. "Now free me."

Nathan approached slowly. "I can pray with you. I can—"

"I didn't ask for prayer."

He surged forward—not with a weapon, but with a scream of brokenness that tore from his throat like something long caged.

Nathan stopped him instantly—not by force, but by presence. A holy stillness bloomed outward from Nathan's stance, freezing the man mid-step, the air around him thickening with peace so tangible it felt like a wall.

Tyler inhaled sharply. "Papa…"

Nathan touched the man's forehead—gentle, steady. "God sees your pain," he whispered. "Every wound. Every night you waited in the dark. But if you want freedom, you must choose it. He won't force it. He never does."

For a moment, the descendant's expression softened—a flicker of the boy he once was, small and hopeful, before the world broke him. But just as quickly, he tore himself backward.

"You will regret denying me power," he spat, retreating into the shadows of the palms.

Tyler clung to Nathan as the man ran off away from them, ranting and raving.

"Why didn't he want to be helped?"

Nathan sighed softly, arm still around his son. "Some people fear freedom more than chains. The unknown feels scarier than the cage they know."

Once the tribespeople were safely transported, Liora approached with a final scroll, hands trembling slightly. "This," she said, "is the story of the Keeper's Mark."

Nathan unrolled it. The painting matched Tyler's vision exactly: a boy standing defiant in a storm, hand outstretched, a glowing flame encircled on his forearm—bright, living, calling.

"He is a child of the East Wind," Liora explained. "His line guarded the ancient knowledge through every scattering. He will open paths no one else can."

"But he is alone," Tyler whispered, voice small but certain. "I saw it. He's waiting for someone to come. For us."

Nathan touched his son's shoulder, feeling the quiet strength already growing there. "Then we will go to him."

They boarded the reinforced rover-ship—engines purring low as it skimmed over the waves. The sky was soft gray, threaded with the first hints of the Eastern storm line—dark clouds gathering like a promise and a warning.

Tyler dropped into the seat beside Nathan—not with the boyish flop of years past, but with the posture of someone who wanted to be taken seriously. His legs were longer now, shoulders unsettled in that tender in-between of not-child, not-man. He exhaled sharply and turned toward Nathan.

"Haba…" he began, the new title carrying weight—respect, love, recognition. "Before we get there, I need to tell you everything."

Nathan's chest warmed, a quiet joy blooming beneath the gravity of the moment. "I'm listening."

Tyler nodded once, gathering his thoughts like he'd been trained—steady, deliberate.

"Okay—first: Master Siyah says my perception is sharpening. Sometimes I pick up on people's feelings before they say anything. Not like I hear them… more like I sense what they're trying not to show. The hurt they hide. The hope they're afraid to name."

Nathan raised an eyebrow, genuinely impressed. "That's emotional discernment. A gift. And a responsibility."

Tyler shrugged modestly. "I'm still learning to control it. Daro taught me breathing patterns so I don't get overwhelmed. He said a leader can't make choices in panic. He said I have to learn to breathe with God before I speak for our people."

Nathan smiled softly. "That sounds like Daro."

Tyler went on, warming to the topic, voice gaining strength. "And I learned some of the Western Wind rituals—the real ones, not the ones tied to the fake sea spirit. Liora taught me this prayer they say before big decisions. It asks God to quiet the storms inside us so we can hear Him better. I've been saying it every morning."

Nathan's eyes softened with pride, seeing the young man emerging from the boy.

Tyler hesitated before continuing. "And the visions…" He swallowed. "They don't terrify me anymore. I'm starting to understand that they're not punishments—they're assignments. God's trying to show me things. Prepare me. Guide me."

Nathan leaned closer, giving him space to speak.

Tyler's voice lowered, intimate. "I know I'm supposed to lead someday. Not now—but someday. So, I've been trying to take things more seriously. Watching how you carry everything. How do you stay calm even when everything's falling apart? How do you not lose yourself when things get… intense. How you always point back to God, no matter what."

Nathan blinked, touched to his core, throat tightening.

Tyler looked away, suddenly embarrassed. "Sorry. That probably sounded dumb."

"No," Nathan whispered, voice thick. "That sounded like a young man learning wisdom. And it means more than you know."

Tyler's shoulders eased. "And the responsibilities?" Nathan asked gently.

Tyler nodded slowly. "I know people will depend on me. And I want to honor God… and Dad… and you, Haba. I don't want to disappoint anyone. I want to be ready."

Nathan's heart squeezed with emotion—pride, tenderness, a fierce protectiveness mixed with deep trust.

"You're growing beautifully," he said. "You're stepping into who God is shaping you to be. And you're doing it with humility. That's rarer than any gift."

Tyler's face broke into a hopeful smile—bright, unguarded. "Haba… do you really think I can help with the Eastern Tribe challenge?"

Nathan wrapped an arm around him—not as protection, but as acknowledgment of the man he was becoming.

"I don't think it," Nathan said. "I know it."

Tyler's breath hitched softly—hope blooming bright across his face, eyes shining. "Thank you, Haba."

Nathan didn't need to speak. He simply held his son as the Eastern coastline rose from the storm-flecked horizon—dark clouds parting just enough to reveal jagged stone and the faint outline of an ancient gateway.

Tyler looked forward—not as a frightened child, but as an heir stepping toward destiny, shoulders squared, heart open.

As the coastline of the Eastern lands rose through the fog, Nathan stood at the rail.

"These people are storm-born," he told Tyler. "They guard their borders with trials—tests that break or forge."

"What kind of trial?" Tyler asked, voice steady.

Nathan smiled faintly. "The kind that tests the heart. The kind you're ready for."

Tyler drew in a breath—not afraid, but determined, the Keeper's Mark still burning behind his eyes.

The storm clouds parted fully over the coastline, revealing the ancient stone gateway of the East Wind Tribe—tall, weathered, waiting.

Their challenge awaited. And Tyler stepped forward—ready.

(19) Storm Before the Threshold

The sea had gone strangely still—too still.

The reinforced hovercraft skimmed across the glassy surface toward the storm-wreathed coastline of the Eastern Tribes, engines thrumming low, almost reverent, as though the water itself were listening. The horizon ahead was a bruise of slate and charcoal, clouds coiled like serpents waiting to strike. Then the engines coughed once—sharply, unwillingly—sputtered like a heart skipping, and died completely.

The craft drifted, momentum bleeding away until it sat motionless on the mirror-flat water, rocking gently in a silence that felt deliberate.

Nathan felt the shift instantly—not mechanical, but spiritual. A cold weight settled in the air, the same oppressive heaviness he'd sensed from the bitter descendant on the beach. The atmosphere thickened, pressing against skin and lungs like the prelude to a scream.

Tyler gripped the railing, knuckles whitening. "Haba… something's wrong."

Nathan nodded, eyes scanning the mist that had begun to rise behind them. "Yes. He's back."

A shape coalesced from the fog—a small, battered skiff cutting through the stillness with unnatural purpose. The same man, the same hollow eyes, but colder now, darker, as though the storm itself had taken root inside his chest and grown roots. His face was gaunt, shadowed by days without sleep, yet his gaze burned with a focused, dangerous hunger.

The skiff scraped against their hull with a low, grating kiss. The man stepped aboard without invitation, boots thudding on the deck, unsteady confidence in every movement.

Tyler instinctively moved behind Nathan, breath shallow.

The man sneered, lips curling back from teeth. "You thought saving them made you a hero, Firebearer. But you left me in the dark."

Nathan kept his voice even, calm as deep water. "You refused healing. You turned away from God's offer."

"I didn't ask for His light!" the man snapped, voice cracking with raw fury. "I asked for power. And you denied me. Again."

His bitterness pulsed outward, filling the air with an oppressive heaviness that made the hovercraft creak on its hull, as though the vessel itself recoiled. The mist thickened around them, coiling like smoke from a dying fire.

Tyler's breath tightened. "Haba… I can feel his anger. It's… heavy."

"Yes," Nathan murmured, never taking his eyes from the man. "Don't fear it. Discern it."

Nathan stepped forward—one hand behind him, palm open in silent reassurance to Tyler.

"Listen to me," Nathan said gently. "Anger is not strength. Woundedness is not authority. If you keep feeding this darkness, it will consume you—until there's nothing left to save."

The man snarled, stepping closer. "I don't need your sermons. I need what's hidden in the East. And I will take it."

He lunged—not with a blade, but with the full weight of his brokenness, hands outstretched as though to seize something invisible.

Nathan did not draw his sword. Instead, he raised one hand—calm, steady, an anchor in chaos.

"Tyler," Nathan said softly, eyes still locked on the man, "what do we do when darkness confronts us?"

Tyler swallowed hard, heart hammering, but he stepped forward—not behind Nathan, but beside him.

"We don't fear it," Tyler answered, voice trembling but firm. "We don't fight with our strength. We stand in God's authority."

"Good," Nathan whispered. "Show me."

Tyler lifted his chin, eyes bright with the fire that had been growing in him since the island. "You don't belong to this tribe," he said to the man. "You don't have authority here. And you cannot stop what God is doing."

The words rang out—clear, spiritual truth cutting through the heaviness like a bell in fog. The man hesitated—not because of Nathan, but because Tyler's voice carried the unmistakable ring of innocence aligned with divine certainty. Something flickered across the man's face: confusion, fear, a fleeting glimpse of the longing he had buried long ago.

Nathan placed a steadying hand on his son's shoulder. "Now," he said quietly, "speak freedom, not fury."

Tyler drew in a shaky breath. "God wants to heal you," he said, voice gaining strength. "He sees every scar, every night you waited alone. But you have to want it. We won't force you. We won't fight you. But we won't follow you."

The corrupted descendant staggered backward, expression fracturing—just for a moment—into something almost human: the boy he had been before exile twisted him. Then he tore himself away, retreating to his skiff.

"This isn't finished," he hissed, voice thick with rage and something deeper—grief.

He vanished into the mist.

The moment he was gone, the engines hummed back to life—soft at first, then steady, as though the sea itself exhaled in relief.

But they didn't get far.

The horizon split open with thunder. Black clouds rolled toward them at impossible speed, spiraling into a monstrous storm wall that swallowed the sky. Lightning forked inside it, illuminating shapes that were not clouds—coiled, serpentine, hungry.

Nathan gritted his teeth. "This isn't a coincidence. The East is guarding its territory."

Waves surged, white-capped and furious. Wind howled, whipping salt spray across the deck. The hovercraft bucked violently, hull slamming against rising swells.

"Haba, what do we do?" Tyler yelled over the roaring wind.

"We wait it out," Nathan decided, voice carrying above the gale. "To force our way through would be disrespectful. And dangerous."

They anchored near a jagged outcrop of black rock, securing the vessel with reinforced tethers that groaned under the strain. Inside the cabin, the storm shattered against the hull like war drums, relentless, testing.

Nathan pulled Tyler close on the bench seat, arm around his shoulders. "Rest while you can," he murmured. "We'll need it."

Tyler nodded, head resting against Nathan's shoulder, exhaustion creeping in despite the adrenaline. Nathan whispered a prayer over him—simple, steady words of protection, guidance, peace—until the storm swallowed the night.

Meanwhile, back at the new tribal center, Gabriel landed his tenth trip of the day.

The construction site was no longer a dream—it was an empire awakening. Housing blocks rose in neat terraces along the valley slopes, stone and timber blending with living green. Agricultural paddocks thrived under new irrigation channels, green shoots pushing through rich soil. Hunters formed cooperative guilds, sharing knowledge once hoarded. Waste management systems—simple, elegant, sustainable—were fully functional. Guardians trained future scouts on the high ridges, silhouettes sharp against the sunset. The healing pavilion had expanded three times its original size, white curtains fluttering in the breeze, soft voices singing inside. Children played freely on sacred ground that had once been shadowed, laughter ringing like bells.

More people arrived hourly—drawn by the universal beacon that vibrated through spiritual bloodlines, through dreams, through whispers carried on the wind.

Gabriel's wrist communicator flashed the newest count: 1,330 souls —130 from the Western Wind today—and climbing weekly.

He snapped photos from the balcony overlooking the valley—families settling into new homes, elders teaching children the old songs with new joy, smoke rising from communal fires—and sent them to Nathan with captions: "The tribe is real." "We are building a city." "They're learning to love one another again."

He stood there a long moment, wind moving through his hair, heart swelling with hope so fierce it ached.

"Not bad," he murmured to the valley, to the sky, to the God who had called them all home, "for a people scattered for centuries."

Back on the hovercraft, the storm raged on through the night—testing, shaping, preparing.

And in the quiet between thunderclaps, father and son rested—together—knowing the dawn would bring the true trial.

The East Wind waited. And they would answer.

The hovercraft skimmed low across the final stretch of restless sea, engines humming down to a reverent whisper as the storm—once a howling wall of gray fury—finally relented. Winds gentled to a soft caress, carrying the clean, metallic scent of rain-soaked stone and distant cedar. Clouds parted like torn silk, strips of early morning light spilling through in pale gold, gilding the waves and turning the horizon into a living edge of fire and promise.

Nathan nudged Tyler awake with a gentle hand on his shoulder. "It's time," he said softly, voice low with the weight of arrival.

Tyler stirred, rubbed sleep from his eyes, and pushed himself upright in the seat. He blinked once, twice—then his breath caught, sharp and audible.

Before them rose the cliffs of the Eastern Tribe.

They were not merely tall; they were sovereign. Black basalt and storm-scarred granite thrust upward from the sea like the spine of some ancient leviathan, sheer faces rising hundreds of feet, crowned by jagged spires that pierced the lingering mist. Ancient spirals—deeply incised, weathered but still sharp—curved across the rock in rhythmic patterns: symbols of wind, lightning, unbroken cycles, endurance. In places, the carvings caught the new light and seemed to breathe, shadows shifting as though the stone itself remembered every gale it had withstood.

Mist rolled over the lower cliffs in slow, thick drifts, curling like the breath of a sleeping titan, veiling and revealing in the same breath. From hidden grottos high above, faint waterfalls threaded down the rock face, silver threads that caught the sunrise and shattered into prismatic sparks before disappearing into the sea below.

At the base of the cliffs, a narrow crescent of black-sand beach curved protectively, dotted with weathered stone sentinels—monoliths half-buried, etched with the same spirals, standing like silent wardens. Beyond the beach, a single, massive stone archway rose from the sand: ancient, unyielding, its curve framed by twin pillars carved with interlocking flames and storm clouds. The arch was not ornate; it was elemental—power made simple, endurance made visible.

A narrow path of worn stone steps, slick with spray, climbed from the beach through the arch and vanished into the mist-shrouded heights. Somewhere above, unseen, the true village waited—carved into the cliffs, sheltered by the very stone that guarded it.

Tyler pressed a palm to the hovercraft's window, eyes wide, chest rising and falling in quick, shallow breaths. The vision from the estate bedroom—the child, the mark, the storm—had been vivid, but this… this was real. The air coming through the vents carried salt, wet rock, ozone, and something deeper: the faint, clean hum of a place that had waited, generation after generation, for the right moment.

Nathan placed a steady hand on Tyler's back, feeling the quick flutter of his son's heartbeat through the fabric. "Welcome," he said quietly, almost reverently, "to the land of the East Wind."

Tyler exhaled hard, steadying himself. His fingers curled against the glass for a moment longer, as though anchoring himself to the sight. Then he turned to Nathan, eyes bright—not with fear, but with the fierce, quiet certainty that had been growing in him for months.

"I'm ready," he whispered.

And for the first time—truly, bone-deep—Nathan believed him.

He saw it in the set of Tyler's shoulders, no longer hunched with the uncertainty of youth. He saw it in the way Tyler's gaze lingered on the arch, not shrinking from its scale but measuring it, accepting it. He saw it in the small, determined lift of his chin—the same lift Nathan had once felt in himself when the first call came.

The hovercraft settled gently onto the black sand, hull kissing the shore with barely a sound. The engines sighed to silence. Outside, the mist drifted, parting just enough to reveal the first few steps of the ascending path.

Nathan rose first, offering his hand. Tyler took it—not because he needed steadying, but because he wanted to walk this together.

They stepped out into the cool, salt-heavy air. The wind touched their faces—strong but no longer hostile, carrying the faint echo of distant thunder and the promise of something vast waiting above.

Tyler looked up the long climb, then back at Nathan. A small, brave smile broke across his face. "Lead the way, Haba."

Nathan returned the smile, pride, and tenderness warring in his chest. "No," he said softly. "This time… we walk side by side."

Together they started up the ancient steps, the stone warm beneath their feet despite the morning chill, each tread carrying them higher—toward the child who waited, toward the mark that called, toward the next chapter of a destiny that had been written long before either of them was born.

The East Wind Tribe's gateway loomed above. And Tyler—
once a boy, now an heir—stepped forward, ready.

(20) The Trial of the Storm and the Fire

The hovercraft settled onto the narrow shingle beach with a soft hiss, its engines winding down into silence. The air was thick with salt and the low growl of distant thunder. Nathan stepped out first, boots crunching on wet pebbles, then turned to offer a hand to Tyler. The rest of the small team—Talem, a few warriors, and Liora's chosen elders—followed, their faces etched with quiet determination.

Nathan scanned the jagged coastline ahead. The cliffs rose like the spine of some ancient beast, wind-scoured and relentless. Behind his wise, steady gaze, the stones seemed to shimmer— not with ordinary light, but with echoes of time. He saw flashes: ancient peoples slipping through hidden passages for shelter during tempests, families carving out lives in the rock, warriors standing guard against both storm and shadow. He saw their spiritual battles too—their cries to the One True God, the false whispers of chaos spirits, the moments of refuge and deliverance.

He exhaled slowly, the weight of it settling in his chest.

"Time is escaping fast," Nathan said, voice low but carrying over the wind. "There's still so much to discover, so many branches yet to gather. We need to move Northward—toward the North Tribe—without delay."

The team nodded, already reaching for packs and gear.

Nathan placed a hand on Talem's shoulder. "You lead them onward. Begin the journey. Tyler and I will catch up."

Talem frowned. "You're not coming with us?"

"I can fly," Nathan reminded him gently. "We'll close the distance quickly. But right now…I sense something personal and timely here in the East. A deal that requires only the two of us. Each of us has specific duties to accomplish before the greater gathering."

The team exchanged glances, then bowed their heads in acceptance. Within minutes, they were moving—packs shouldered, a quiet line disappearing up the winding coastal path toward the northern horizon.

Nathan watched them go until they were specks against the gray stone. Then he turned to Tyler.

The boy's eyes were wide, but not with fear—anticipation flickered there, tempered by the maturity he'd been growing into.

"Ready, Haba?" Tyler asked.

Nathan smiled faintly. "Always, when I'm with you."

They started up the trail alone.

The cliffs grew more daunting with every step. Wind-swept stone towers rose on either side, dense and rugged. Jagged rocks, carved by eternal storms into impossible shapes, loomed overhead. Through Nathan's discerning sight, faint glows traced ancient carvings—runes of protection, warnings, and remembrance.

 Tyler walked close beside him. Every few minutes, he glanced up.

"Haba… can you sense it? What we're walking into?"

Nathan nodded. "I can. A young voice. A boy's thoughts are quiet but strong. His name is Souta. It means 'Sudden Thick Peace' in the old tongue."

Tyler's breath caught. "I hear him, too. Like whispers on the wind. He's… waiting. But he's afraid."

They continued in silence until the path split—two narrow trails diverging like veins in stone.

A sudden storm cloud descended without warning. It boiled down from the sky, swallowing the light, wrapping them in swirling darkness. Thunder cracked close enough to rattle their bones.

Tyler stumbled backward, boots scraping against wet stone, eyes blown wide with primal terror. The visions crashed over him like breaking surf—true and false tangled in a merciless flood:

- Souta, tiny and shivering, curled in the black belly of a cave, whispering *"Tyler... where are you?"* into endless dark.
- The whole tribe rushing forward, arms open, faces bright with tears of welcome.
- Nathan swallowed by blinding white light, gone in an instant, leaving only scorched earth behind.
- The empire rising, glorious—then crumbling in the same heartbeat, ash raining like gentle snow.
- A smiling false peace that stretched too wide, too thin, until it swallowed the sky whole.

The boy gasped, small hands clamping over his temples as though he could physically hold his mind together. "Haba—*it's too much!*" His voice cracked high and raw. "They're screaming—all of them at once—I can't—I can't tell which one is real!"

Nathan stood untouched. The illusions broke and slid off him like rain on oiled canvas; the spiritual mantle he carried—quiet, unshowy, but ironclad—held firm. Yet inside, a voice older than the cliffs themselves spoke without sound: *Encourage, do not steer. This crucible belongs to him. He must prove his right to*

*lead—not through strength, not through cleverness, but through
naked trust in the still, small chime of truth amid the roar.*

Nathan sank slowly to one knee, bringing himself level with the
trembling child. His voice came low and warm, steady as a
hearth fire in winter. "Breathe with me, sweetheart. Just like
Daro showed you. In… through the nose… hold… out the mouth.
First with God, then with fear. Let the fear come. Let it sit beside
you. But don't give it the reins."

Tyler's chest heaved in ugly, hiccupping bursts. Tears carved
clean tracks through the dust on his cheeks. "But what if I pick
the wrong one?" he whispered. "What if I choose the lie and I
lead everyone straight into—into nothing? The tribe, Souta,
you… What if I *fail* them, Nathan? All of them?"

Nathan's hand hovered near Tyler's shoulder—close enough to
feel the heat of the boy's panic, but not touching. Not yet. "You
already asked for wisdom, remember? Back on the ridge when
the wind was trying to steal your breath. You asked, and He
answered. That answer is already inside you." A small, almost
shy smile touched his mouth. "It's not about being fearless. It's
about being afraid *and still listening.* I'm right here, Ty. But this
part… this step… You have to take it alone."

The storm tightened around them, a living gray throat closing.
Nathan's voice grew thin, fraying at the edges, until it was only
a distant echo threading through the roar: *"…trust…the
chime…always…"*

And then he was gone. The cloud swallowed Tyler whole.

Loneliness hit harder than any vision—cold, bottomless,
personal. He dropped to his knees, palms slapping wet rock. His
whole body shook so violently that his teeth clacked. *God…* The
word was more breath than prayer. *I'm so scared. I don't want
to run anymore, but I don't know how to stay. Please. Help me*

see. Help me choose the real one. I don't want to be the boy who ruins everything.

He squeezed his eyes shut. Forced the breaths Daro had drilled into him until they hurt: In… "Wisdom…" Out… "Wisdom…" In… "Please… wisdom…"

Slowly—agonizingly—the chaos began to thin, like ink bleeding out of wet paper.

One image steadied and grew solid: Souta at the village mouth, small bare feet planted, chin lifted, hand raised high—not in surrender, but in welcome. The boy's eyes were bright, trusting, alive.

Another flickered beside it, seductive: the same Souta turning away, shoulders hunched, face shadowed with betrayal. *You left me,* the false vision whispered. *You always leave.*

Tyler locked onto the first image. He waited, barely daring to breathe. Then it came—a single, crystalline *chime*, pure as mountain spring water tapped once with silver. The false vision fractured like cheap glass, edges curling into smoke.

He opened his eyes. The storm cloud flinched as though struck, then tore apart in ragged gray wisps that fled upward into the wind.

Nathan was there again—had he ever truly left?—watching with quiet, fierce pride in his eyes. "You did it," he said, voice soft enough to break. "You really did it."

Tyler launched himself forward like a released arrow. His arms locked around Nathan's ribs in a desperate, crushing hug. "I was *so* scared," he sobbed into the man's coat. "I thought I was going to lose you—lose *everything*—but I heard it. I heard the chime. I chose right."

Nathan folded around him, one broad hand cradling the back of Tyler's head, the other steady between his shoulder blades. "You were never alone, little fire," he murmured into the boy's hair. "Not for one heartbeat. And now you know it here—" he tapped Tyler's chest gently "—not just here." He touched the boy's temple.

They stayed like that a long minute, wind gentling, world quieting, until Tyler finally leaned back, scrubbing his face with both sleeves. His eyes were red-rimmed but brighter, steadier.

"I'm ready now," he said, voice still wobbly but certain. "For whatever comes next. Really ready."

Nathan studied him a moment longer, then nodded once. "Then let's go meet Souta."

They followed the true path—the one marked by faint, living glows that pulsed like heartbeats—for another twenty minutes. The trail finally opened into a sheltered bowl of stone. Weathered huts of gray rock clustered together like old friends leaning on one another. Only the silver-haired ones moved here—slow, deliberate, tending tiny gardens of hardy greens, mending nets, humming wordless tunes to the cliffs themselves.

Later, they would learn the young warriors and hunters lived in the high cliff dwellings and hidden outposts that ringed the valley—eyes always outward, spears always near.

But here, in the quiet heart of the village, the next trial waited. Not for Tyler. For the Foreign Fire.

An elder woman rose from a low bench of carved stone. Time had etched deep rivers across her face, yet her eyes burned clear and unsparing. They fixed on Nathan alone.

"You carry the flame," she said. The words were neither question nor accusation—simply fact. "But fire alone does not make a son of the center. Allegiance is not inherited. It is forged. The old tribe calls you home, Foreign Fire. Prove you are truly of us… or the East Wind will stay shut to you forever."

Nathan inclined his head, slow and respectful. "I am ready," he answered.

The trial of the Foreign Fire had begun.

(21) The Fire Proved

The elder woman—her name was Mara, Keeper of the East Wind Threshold—stood motionless before Nathan, her silver braids whipping in the sudden gust that swept through the village square. The elderly villagers had gathered in a wide semicircle, silent, their weathered faces unreadable. Every eye rested on the Foreign Fire.

Mara lifted one gnarled hand. From the stone bench where she had been seated rose a low, resonant hum. The ground beneath Nathan's feet trembled—not violently, but deeply, as though the cliffs themselves were waking to judge him.

"You carry flame," Mara said, her voice cutting through the wind like a blade. "But flame can burn friend and foe alike. The old tribe demands more than light. It demands proof of allegiance. Proof of lineage. Proof that your heart belongs to the center, not to yourself."

Nathan bowed his head once, slowly.

"I submit," he answered. "Test me as the Almighty wills."

The hum intensified.

Without warning, the sky above the village darkened—not with storm clouds, but with a sudden, unnatural twilight. Shadows poured down the cliffs like ink, coiling around Nathan's ankles, climbing his legs, pressing against his chest. They were not mere darkness; they were memories—living, accusing memories of every moment the scattered tribes had suffered while the world forgot them.

He saw:

- Children weeping in hidden caves while storms raged overhead

159

- Warriors dying on foreign shores, their last breath a prayer no one heard
- Elders carving warnings into stone that the coming generations would never read
- A people enslaved twice—once by chains, once by silence

The weight of it crushed inward. Nathan staggered to one knee. The shadows whispered:

You were not here. You lived in comfort while we bled. Your fire is late. Too late. Why should we trust a stranger now?

Sweat broke across Nathan's brow. His breath came shallow. The spiritual pressure was immense—far heavier than the sea spirit on the Western island. This was not deception; this was righteous accusation. The East Wind had borne centuries of isolation, and now it demanded an accounting.

Tyler, standing several paces back among the elders, clenched his fists. His eyes filled, but he did not move. He understood— this trial was Nathan's alone.

Nathan's chest heaved. He could feel the armor of God flickering around him, ready to flare, ready to defend. But something deeper restrained him. A quiet knowing.

Not yet.

He lifted his face toward the darkened sky, arms spreading wide.

"Almighty God," he cried, voice steady even as the shadows tightened, "King of Heaven and Earth, Father of the scattered and the found—I call upon You now."

Silence swallowed the square.

Then Nathan's voice rose again, clear and resolute.

"Before I ask anything for myself, I ask for them. Pour out Your favor upon this village. Let Your blessing rest upon every elder who has guarded the threshold through storm and silence. Let Your provision flow into their gardens, Your peace into their hearts, Your healing into their bones. Let the children yet unborn know that You have not forgotten the East Wind. Let them rise in strength and joy because You are faithful."

A soft warmth brushed the square.

One by one, the elders felt it—first as a breeze, then as sunlight breaking through closed eyelids. A single tear slipped down Mara's cheek. An old man leaned on his staff and smiled for the first time in years. A woman pressed trembling hands to her chest as though breathing fresh air after decades underwater.

The shadows around Nathan hesitated.

Only then did Nathan continue, voice lower, intimate, yet carrying the same unshakable authority.

"And now, Lord… grant me spiritual authority to walk here in grace and peace. Not for my glory. Not to prove myself greater. But so that I may serve these Your people, so that I may carry the flame without burning the fragile, so that the lineage may be restored in truth and love. Let my steps be ordered by You. Let my words carry Your weight. Let my heart remain humble before You and before them."

The warmth that had touched the elders now surged toward Nathan.

Light—pure, white, living—erupted from within him. Not the blazing holy fire of battle, but a steady, radiant glow, like dawn rising inside a man. The shadows recoiled, shrieking faintly, then dissolved like mist before sunrise.

The unnatural twilight lifted.

Sunlight—real, golden—poured over the village once more.

Mara stepped forward slowly. Her eyes, once hard as flint, now shimmered with something softer.

She reached out and laid both hands upon Nathan's shoulders.

"The fire has been proved," she whispered. "Not by power. But by love first. You asked blessing for us before you asked for strength for yourself. That is the mark of true lineage. That is the heart of the center."

Behind her, the elders began to kneel—not in fear, but in reverence.

One by one they touched their foreheads to the ground, murmuring prayers in the old tongue.

Tyler rushed forward and wrapped his arms around Nathan's waist, face buried against his side.

Nathan rested one hand on the boy's head, the other still open toward heaven.

"Thank You," he breathed. "Thank You."

Mara straightened, wiping her eyes with the edge of her shawl.

"Come," she said. "The village welcomes you both. And tonight… we will bring Souta to you. The boy with the mark has waited long enough."

Nathan nodded, chest rising and falling with quiet awe.

The Foreign Fire had passed through the fire.

And the East Wind had begun to open.

As the sun dipped low over the jagged cliffs, painting the village in hues of amber and rose, the elders gathered once more in the central square. A simple feast had been laid out—fresh-caught fish grilled over open flames, root vegetables seasoned with wild herbs, and flatbreads baked in stone ovens. The air carried the scent of salt and smoke, mingling with the faint hum of evening prayers.

Tyler sat beside Nathan on a woven mat, his earlier triumph in the storm cloud still glowing in his cheeks. The boy fidgeted slightly, eyes darting toward the cliff dwellings where shadows lengthened. "Haba… do you think Souta knows we're here? I can still hear his thoughts—curious ones, like he's wondering about everything."

Nathan smiled softly, placing a reassuring hand on Tyler's shoulder. "He knows. And soon, you'll meet him."

Mara approached, her steps measured, a small figure trailing behind her like a shadow come to life. The boy was no more than eight or nine, slight of build with sun-kissed skin and dark hair that fell in wild curls over his forehead. His eyes—wide, deep brown, and shimmering with unspoken questions—locked first on Tyler.

Souta stopped short, tilting his head. A shy grin broke across his face, pure and unguarded. "You're… like me? Not old like the elders. Can we play? I know a secret path up the cliffs where the wind sings. No one else goes there 'cause it's too high, but I bet you could climb it!"

Tyler blinked, then laughed—a bright, genuine sound that cut through the evening hush. "Yeah! I'd love that. I'm Tyler. What's the wind sound like when it sings?"

Souta's eyes lit up, his small hands gesturing wildly. "Like this—whoooosh, but soft, like a story being told. Come on, I'll show you after!"

But then Souta's gaze shifted to Nathan.

The boy froze, mouth parting in awe. Nathan sat there, his white tunic catching the fading light, his presence radiating that quiet, otherworldly peace that had become his hallmark. Souta took a tentative step forward, then another, drawn like a moth to a gentle flame.

"Are… are you an angel?" Souta whispered, his voice barely above the crackle of the fire. He reached out slowly, fingers brushing the edge of Nathan's robe as if testing if it were real. The fabric shimmered faintly under his touch, and Souta gasped. "It's so soft… like clouds. And your hair—" He stretched up on tiptoes, one small hand gently touching a lock of Nathan's hair, which gleamed in the firelight. "It's like the sun when it breaks through storms. Do angels have hair like that? Why are you here? Did God send you to fix the bad winds? What's it like to fly? I saw you in a dream once, but you were bigger, like a mountain."

The questions tumbled out in a rush, Souta's curiosity spilling over without filter or fear. His purity shone through—innocent wonder wrapped in a child's unscarred heart, untouched by the world's cynicism.

Nathan's breath caught. He knelt down to Souta's level, his eyes softening with a depth of emotion that surprised even him. This boy—so open, so trusting—reminded him of Tyler in those early days, before visions and trials had begun to shape him. But there was something more in Souta: a quiet resilience, a spark of destiny hidden behind the wide-eyed questions.

"No, little one," Nathan said gently, his voice warm and steady. "I'm not an angel. I'm just a man—a husband, a father, a friend to those who need one. But God does send me sometimes, like He sends the rain after a long dry spell. He poured His fire into me so I could help light the way for others."

Souta's fingers lingered on Nathan's robe for a moment longer before pulling back, his brow furrowing in thought. "But… you glow. Not like fireflies, but inside. And the elders say the Keeper's Mark only wakes for someone special. Look—" He rolled up his sleeve, revealing the swirling flame encircled on his forearm. It pulsed faintly now, alive with a soft golden light that hadn't been there before. "It started burning when you came. It never did that before. Does it mean something?"

Nathan reached out carefully, not touching the mark but hovering his hand near it. A faint resonance hummed between them—the Foreign Fire recognizing its kin. "It means everything, Souta. That mark… It's been in your family for generations. Your ancestors were the Keepers—the ones who guarded the old secrets when the tribes scattered. They fled the great captivity with a promise: to hold the flame until the scattered could gather again."

Souta's eyes widend further. "My family? But… I don't have a family. Not anymore. The storms took my parents when I was little. Mara found me in a cave, crying, with the mark already there. She said it chose me. But why me? I'm not strong like the warriors. I just… ask questions. And dream about places I've never seen."

Nathan's heart ached at the boy's words. He cupped Souta's face gently with one hand. "Because God chooses the pure-hearted, Souta. The ones who see wonder in the world. Your parents— they were guardians too. Your father carved paths through the storms to hide our people's scrolls. Your mother sang the old songs that kept the spirits at bay. They passed the mark to you before they were lost, so you could unlock what's next. The mark isn't just a symbol—it's a key. It opens visions, paths, even doors in the stone that lead to the other Winds."

Souta leaned into Nathan's touch, his curiosity blooming into trust. "Will you teach me? About the flame? And God? And… everything?"

Nathan nodded, a faint smile breaking through. "I will. And Tyler here—he'll be your friend, your playmate. You two can climb those cliffs and hear the wind sing together. But remember, Souta: curiosity is a gift. Keep asking. Keep dreaming. That's how the empire rebuilds—not with swords, but with hearts like yours."

Souta beamed, glancing at Tyler with renewed excitement. "Okay! But first… can I touch your hair again? It's like holding sunlight."

Nathan laughed softly—a rare, full sound that warmed the square. "As much as you want, little one."

As the evening deepened, with Souta peppering them with more questions between bites of bread and fish, Nathan felt a quiet certainty settle in his soul. This boy, with his mark and his innocence, was another piece of the promise. And in Souta's pure gaze, Nathan saw a glimpse of the future he was preparing—one that would shine long after his own path diverged.

(22) The Song of the East Wind

The next morning dawned soft and clear, the kind of rare stillness that only came to the East Wind cliffs after a night of fierce weather had spent itself. The air smelled of clean stone and distant sea, and the village stirred slowly—elders tending small fires, children darting between huts with laughter that echoed off the rock faces.

Nathan woke early, as he always did, and found Tyler and Souta already outside the guest dwelling, sitting cross-legged on a flat stone overlooking the narrow trail they had climbed the day before. The two boys were shoulder to shoulder, heads close together, whispering secrets only children can share.

Souta was pointing toward a jagged outcrop high above them. "See that crack? That's where the wind gets trapped and makes the longest note. It sounds like someone singing really far away. I go up there when I'm sad. It always makes me feel better."

Tyler nodded seriously. "I get that. Sometimes when I have too many visions, everything feels loud inside my head. Maybe the wind could help quiet it."

Souta looked at him with sudden wonder. "You have visions too? Like… seeing things before they happen?"

"Sometimes before. Sometimes things that already happened but nobody remembers. It's scary at first, but Haba—Nathan—says they're assignments, not punishments."

Souta's small fingers traced the glowing mark on his forearm. The flame inside the circle pulsed gently, almost in rhythm with his heartbeat. "Mine started doing this when you both came. Before that, it was just a scar. Now it feels… alive. Like it wants to show me something."

Nathan stepped out quietly and leaned against the doorway, content to watch for a moment. The sight of them—two boys from different worlds, already bound by friendship—filled him with a quiet joy that felt like answered prayer.

Souta noticed him first. His face lit up like sunrise. "Nathan! You're awake! Come see! Tyler wants to hear the wind song, but the path is steep. I told him you could probably carry him if he's scared."

Tyler laughed, cheeks pink. "I'm not scared. I just… haven't climbed cliffs like these before."

Nathan walked over and sat beside them, legs dangling over the edge. "Then we'll go together. All three of us. But first—" He looked at Souta. "Tell me more about the mark. What does it feel like when it wakes?"

Souta thought for a moment, chewing his lower lip. "It's warm. Not hot like fire, but… like someone put their hand on my arm and said 'I'm here.' And sometimes I dream about places I've never been. Big stone circles. A mountain that breathes. A city made of light. And there's always a voice that says, 'Keep it safe until the gathering.'"

Nathan's breath caught. He had heard those same phrases in the scrolls from the Western Wind. "The gathering," he repeated softly. "That's what we're doing, Souta. Bringing everyone home."

Souta's eyes grew huge. "Then… Am I part of it? Really?"

"You are," Nathan said. "You're the Keeper. That mark isn't just yours—it belongs to all of us now. And when it's time, you'll show us the next door."

Tyler reached over and gently touched the mark. A faint chime sounded—not loud, but clear—like crystal tapped once. The flame brightened for a heartbeat, then settled.

Souta giggled. "It likes you!"

The three of them sat in companionable silence for a while, watching the sun climb higher. Then Souta stood suddenly, tugging at Nathan's sleeve.

"Come on! The best time to hear the wind song is right now, before the afternoon storms start. And I want to show Tyler the secret cave where I keep my treasures!"

Nathan rose, offering each boy a hand. "Lead the way, Keeper."

They climbed together—Souta scampering ahead like a mountain goat, Tyler following with careful determination, Nathan bringing up the rear, ready to catch either of them if a foot slipped.

Halfway up, Souta paused at a narrow ledge and cupped his hands around his mouth. He let out a long, clear note—high and pure. The wind caught it, carried it into the crack in the rock, and returned it transformed: deeper, layered, almost like a choir singing from far away.

Tyler's mouth fell open. "That's… beautiful."

Souta beamed. "It's the East Wind saying hello."

They reached the secret cave—a small hollow behind a curtain of hanging vines. Inside, Souta had arranged his treasures with the care of someone who had very little and cherished everything: a perfect spiral shell, a piece of sea glass smoothed by years, a feather the color of storm clouds, a tiny carved wooden fish his father had made before he was lost.

And in the very center, on a flat stone, lay a small, ancient scroll—yellowed, fragile, tied with faded gold thread.

Souta picked it up reverently. "Mara gave me this when the mark first glowed. She said only the Keeper can open it. I've been waiting… I think I've been waiting for you."

He looked from Tyler to Nathan, eyes shining with certainty.

Nathan knelt. "Then let's open it together."

Souta placed the scroll in Nathan's hands. The moment Nathan's fingers touched it, the flame on Souta's arm flared bright— golden, steady, alive.

The gold thread loosened on its own.

The scroll unrolled slowly, revealing not words, but a map.

A map of swirling winds—North, South, East, West— converging toward a single glowing point at the center.

And beneath it, in elegant script older than the cliffs themselves:

"When the Keeper's flame joins the Foreign Fire, the path to the Great Center shall be revealed. But beware: the shadow that was denied will rise again. Only the pure heart can stand against it."

Tyler's hand found Nathan's. Souta's small fingers slipped into Nathan's other palm.

For a long moment, none of them spoke.

Then Souta whispered, "We're going to the center, aren't we?"

Nathan looked down at the two boys—one already proven in trial, the other marked by destiny—and felt the weight of promise settle over them like a mantle.

"Yes," he said softly. "We are."

And somewhere deep in the cliffs, the wind sang again—not in warning, but in welcome.

The gathering had truly begun.

The cave's quiet lingered long after the scroll had been read, its ancient words hanging in the air like a promise yet to be fulfilled. Nathan carefully rolled it back up, tying the gold thread with deliberate care, while Souta and Tyler peered over his shoulders, their faces a mix of awe and excitement.

"This map," Nathan said softly, "it's more than lines on parchment. It's the heartbeat of our people. The Great Center—it's where everything began, and where it must end. Or begin again."

Souta's small hand tightened around the feather from his treasures. "Does that mean... we have to leave? The village? The cliffs?"

Nathan met his gaze steadily. "Not alone. And not forever. But yes, little one. The gathering calls us all."

They descended the path in thoughtful silence, the wind song fading behind them as the village came back into view. By midday, the elders had convened in the square, Mara at their center, her voice carrying with the authority of one who had guarded these cliffs for decades.

"The Foreign Fire has spoken," she announced to the gathered villagers—elders, warriors descending from the cliff dwellings, families with wide-eyed children. "The Keeper's mark has awakened. The scroll reveals the path. We must prepare for the pilgrimage—to the gathering spot where the heir awaits, where the tribes unite under God's hand."

A murmur rippled through the crowd, not of fear, but of anticipation. Packs were assembled swiftly: dried fish and roots bundled in woven nets, sacred carvings wrapped in soft hides, water skins filled from the cliff springs. Warriors sharpened their spears, not for battle, but for protection on the long journey ahead. Children helped where they could, tying knots and whispering prayers.

Souta clung close to Tyler as the preparations unfolded. "You'll stay with me, right? On the way?"

Tyler grinned, slinging an arm around the younger boy's shoulders. "Of course. We're friends now. And Haba—Nathan—he'll watch over us both."

Nathan stood a little apart, his eyes scanning the horizon. He felt the pull—the inexorable draw toward the center—but also the shadow. It was closer now, that final evil presence he had glimpsed in visions. His time was imminent; he knew it in his bones, in the faint tremor that sometimes ran through his hands after wielding the fire. But he would not speak of it yet. Not to the boys.

As the sun climbed higher, a distant hum echoed from the northern trail—the sound of approaching footsteps and voices. The other party had arrived: Talem at the lead, with Liora's elders and the Western Wind warriors who had pressed onward the day before. Their faces were weathered from the road, but lit with purpose.

"We've reached the Northern Tribe," Talem reported, bowing slightly to Nathan. "They're a hardy people—ice-carvers, guardians of the frozen winds. They felt the call, just as the scroll predicted. Even now, they're gathering their clans, preparing to join the pilgrimage. But they need a sign—a flame to melt the doubt in their hearts."

Nathan nodded. "The sign will come. Tell them the Foreign Fire walks with them, and the Keeper's mark lights the way."

Talem's eyes flickered to Souta, who straightened under the gaze, the mark on his arm glowing faintly. "We will. And we'll escort as many as can travel south, to the gathering spot."

As the group integrated, sharing stories and supplies, Nathan felt a familiar brush against his mind—Gabriel's voice, steady and warm, like a hand on his shoulder across the miles.

Nathan... love. How goes the East?

Nathan closed his eyes, leaning into the connection. *Fruitful. The boy—Souta—he's the Keeper we've sought. Pure-hearted, marked by destiny. He'll come with us, with Tyler. The village prepares to make a pilgrimage to you now.*

A pause, then Gabriel's thoughts flooded with images and updates from the homefront—the tribal center, alive and expanding under his watchful eye.

The gathering swells, Gabriel shared. *More arrive daily— scattered branches from forgotten lines, drawn by the beacon in the cavern. We've broken ground on new homes: sturdy lodges above ground for the elders, woven from cliff vines and blessed timber. On the ground, epicenters rise—great halls for council and worship, ringed by gardens that bloom even in winter. Shopping centers too, simple markets where artisans trade relics and fresh goods. And below... the cavern expands. Tunnels carved into living centers, safe from storms, lit by the ancient wards. Families settle there, their laughter echoing like music. The count is over two thousand now, Nathan. A city reborn. But it waits for you—for all of you.*

Nathan's heart swelled with pride, but a shadow tempered it. He confided then, his thoughts raw and quiet. *Gabriel... the three of us—Tyler, Souta, and I—we must go to the Center Tribe soon. The map calls us there. But I sense... this is the path to my final steps.*

Gabriel's response came sharply, laced with quiet fear. *What do you mean?*

My time is imminent, Nathan admitted. *Another evil presence stirs—the shadow that was denied, the one from the islands, twisted further by bitterness. It will be my final battle. I've seen it, Gabriel. God victorious, as always. But in this clash... He gives a final draw to the remaining hearts, calling them home. And at the same time... He claims me to my final home above.*

Silence stretched across the link, heavy with unspoken grief. Then Gabriel's voice, soft but resolute: *Not yet. Not without me by your side.*

You must stay, Nathan urged. *Lead the gathering. Raise our son. Rebuild what was lost. I prepare the way... You walk it.*

Gabriel's ache echoed back, but so did his love—fierce, unyielding. *Then come home first. Bring the boys. Let us have these days.*

Nathan opened his eyes, the connection fading like a gentle breeze. He looked to Tyler and Souta, now laughing as they helped pack a sled with supplies.

"Soon," he murmured to himself. "But not alone."

The village finished preparations by dusk, and the pilgrimage set to begin at dawn. Fires burned low in the square, stories shared around them—of ancient winds, of flames that freed, of a future bright as the mark on a boy's arm.

Nathan sat with the boys, one on each side, and whispered a prayer into the night.

"Lord... guide our steps. Let the battle be Yours. And if this is my last song... let it echo in their hearts forever."

The wind answered, soft and sure, carrying the promise onward.

(23) The Weight in the Silence

Dawn broke over the cliffs in pale, trembling gold, the light fragile as if it knew the day carried more than sun. The pilgrimage line moved southward in quiet rhythm—litters swaying, children's footsteps pattering, the low murmur of prayers rising like mist. Nathan, Tyler, and Souta walked near the front, the three of them bound by hands and silence that had grown heavier with every mile.

For the first hour, they tried to keep the lightness alive. Souta pointed at seabirds, naming them in the old tongue with forced brightness. Tyler laughed when Souta's imitation of a gull call cracked into a squeak. But the effort showed. And Nathan… Nathan walked with the same steady grace, yet something in him had shifted. His shoulders carried an invisible weight. His eyes, usually so warm when they rested on the boys, held a distant, aching depth—like a man staring across an ocean he knew he would soon cross alone.

Tyler felt it first, a cold knot tightening in his chest. He slowed, tugging Souta to a stop. The younger boy looked up, confused, then followed Tyler's worried gaze to Nathan's face.

"Haba…" Tyler's voice cracked on the word, barely above a whisper. "Please… look at me."

Nathan paused mid-step. The line flowed past them like water around stones. He turned slowly, and when his eyes met Tyler's, they were already glistening.

Tyler's throat worked. "You're… you're carrying something awful. I can feel it. It's all over you. Like the air hurts when you breathe."

Souta's small hand slipped from Tyler's and reached for Nathan's tunic instead, fingers curling into the fabric as if to anchor him. His voice came tiny, trembling. "Your face looks like… like when my mom used to look out at the storm and know it was going to take everything. Haba… are you leaving us? Really leaving?"

The question landed like a stone in still water. Nathan's breath hitched audibly. He knelt right there on the rocky path, knees pressing into the earth, and pulled both boys into his arms without a word. They fit against him perfectly—Souta's head tucked under his chin, Tyler's face buried against his shoulder. For a long moment, no one spoke. Only the wind and the distant crash of waves.

When Nathan finally spoke, his voice was raw, stripped of every layer of calm he usually wore.

"I can't lie to you," he whispered. "Not to either of you. Yes… There's a battle coming. The last one. The shadow that's been following us—the bitterness that turned into something monstrous—it's waiting at the Center. I've seen how it ends. God wins. He always wins. But…" His arms tightened. "But the price… the price might be me."

A sob tore out of Tyler, muffled against Nathan's tunic. "No. No, Haba, you can't. You promised. You said you'd be here. You said we'd do this together—all of us."

Souta's small body shook violently. Tears soaked Nathan's shoulder. "I just got you," he cried. "I lost my mom and dad… I can't lose you too. Please don't go. Please don't leave us alone."

Nathan's own tears fell then—silent, hot, sliding down his cheeks into the boys' hair. He rocked them gently, the way he used to rock Tyler when nightmares came.

"I don't want to leave," he choked out. "God knows I don't. Every part of me wants to stay—wants to see you both grow into the men He's calling you to be, wants to watch you rebuild the empire with your own hands, wants to grow old with your Dad, holding his hand on the balcony while fireworks light up the sky. I want all of it. More than I can say."

He pulled back just enough to cup their faces—one in each hand—so they could see his eyes, red-rimmed and fierce with love.

"But if this is the path He's asking of me… if my life is the final key that opens the door for every scattered heart to come home… then I will walk it. Because I love you too much to refuse what He's asking. Because I trust Him with you more than I trust myself."

Tyler's voice broke into pieces. "We're not ready. I'm not ready. I still need you to tell me when I'm being stupid, or when I'm scared, or… or how to be brave like you."

Souta's sobs came harder. "I need you to teach me the stories. I need you to… to be my Haba too."

Nathan pressed his forehead to theirs, tears mingling. "You'll never be without me. Never. When the moment comes, I'll be closer than your heartbeat. I'll be in every wind that sings on the cliffs, in every flame that lights your way, in every time you choose love over fear. You'll feel me. I swear it."

He kissed Tyler's forehead, then Souta's, lingering on each one. "And until then… we walk this last road together. Every step. Every heartbeat. The three of us. No more hiding the weight. We carry it together."

Tyler clung to him, voice muffled and desperate. "Promise you'll tell us everything. Don't leave us in the dark. Promise."

"I promise," Nathan whispered, voice cracking. "When the time is right, I'll tell you. And I promise this: my last breath will be spent praying for you both. That you'll be strong. That you'll be wise. That you'll love fiercely, the way God loves you."

Souta's small arms wrapped around Nathan's neck. "I love you, Haba. Even if you have to go... I love you forever."

"I love you forever too, little Keeper," Nathan breathed. "Both of you. Forever."

They stayed like that for several long minutes—three hearts pressed together on the edge of the world—until the wind gentled, as if giving them permission to rise.

Nathan stood first, then helped the boys up. Their hands found each other again—fingers laced tight, refusing to let go.

"The Center waits," Nathan said, voice steadier now, though the tears still shone on his cheeks. "And so does the rest of our story. Let's go meet it. Together."

They stepped back onto the path, side by side, the pilgrimage stretching before them like a promise and a farewell woven into one.

The heaviness remained.

But so did the love.

And it burned brighter than any coming shadow.

(24) The Living Breath of Return

Gabriel's POV

On the third day of the East Wind pilgrimage, the tribal center had become something alive—breathing, expanding, unfurling like a great ancient tree under the first true spring sun after endless winter. I felt it in my bones before I saw it: the ground itself hummed with subtle vibration, as though the earth were waking up and stretching after centuries of sleep. The count had reached 3,500 souls—exact tally kept on the massive ledger board in the central hall, updated every dawn by my own hand with a steady stroke and a whispered prayer of thanks that trembled on my lips each time.

They arrived in waves that broke my heart open wider with every crest: small bands from forgotten valleys, lone wanderers drawn by dreams they could not explain, entire clans walking days with children strapped to their backs and elders leaning on carved staffs worn smooth by generations. Each new group was greeted the same way—open arms, warm broth ladled from communal pots, and the same words spoken by every greeter, voice thick with emotion: "You are home. The call has been answered."

I watched from the rise overlooking the main approach, chest tight with joy and a hidden ache that never quite left. Families stumbled into the light of the new fires, eyes wide, tears streaming, dropping to their knees to press palms to the soil as though they needed to feel it was real. Children who had never known more than caves or hidden glens ran barefoot through the paths, laughter ringing like bells against the hills. Elders embraced strangers who carried the same sigils on their mantles, whispering names long thought lost. The air itself seemed saturated with grace—no resentment, no suspicion, only the quiet miracle of reunion.

Construction moved with a swiftness that still stole my breath. No shouted orders. No disputes over placement. No one hoarding tools or claiming the best plots. The people worked as one body—carpenters from the Western Wind patiently teaching their interlocking beam techniques to Northern ice-shapers who had never seen living timber before; Southern weavers braiding ropes alongside Eastern cliff-dwellers who laughed as they learned to knot vines into living walls. Malice had no foothold here. The harmony was palpable, a living thing that moved through the crowd like wind through wheat.

Above ground, the epicenters had multiplied. Three great halls now stood completed—circular, open-roofed in the center so sky and stars could speak directly to every gathering beneath them. Their walls were a mosaic of salvaged stone from ancient ruins, reclaimed timber from fallen giants of the forest, and living vines that had begun to bloom overnight with white star-shaped flowers that glowed faintly in the dark. Between the halls, market squares had bloomed organically: rows of simple stalls offering fresh bread still warm from clay ovens, carved talismans etched with protective sigils, dyed fabrics in colors of every Wind, herbal remedies brewed from newly sprouted plants, and the first fruits of gardens that had been barren earth only days before.

On the ground level, residential rings had formed—clusters of sturdy lodges arranged in gentle spirals that mirrored the sacred patterns on the old archway. Each family received a plot; within hours, walls rose, roofs thatched with woven reed, doorways hung with curtains braided from dyed fibers. The design was intentional: no lodge stood alone. Every home touched at least two others, symbolizing the unbreakable bond of the tribe. Communal fire pits dotted the rings—places where strangers became neighbors over shared meals, stories, and songs that blended old dialects into something new and whole.

Below ground, the ancient cavern had transformed into a vast living center. The wards glowed brighter with each new arrival, illuminating tunnels widened by willing hands. Families claimed chambers carved into the living rock—cool in summer, warm in winter, lit by soft, steady light that needed no flame. Healing alcoves lined one long corridor, where herbalists and prayer warriors worked side by side, hands stained with poultices and oil of anointing. The central underground chamber—large enough for hundreds—had become the heart of worship: smooth stone floor worn by countless footsteps, a raised platform of polished basalt, and walls etched with the sigils of every Wind now present.

I moved through it all like a man carrying both boundless joy and a hidden wound that bled quietly. I rose before first light, walked the perimeter with a lantern, greeted the night watch with a nod and a murmured blessing, then plunged into council after council. Placement teams needed guidance—where to house the incoming Northern ice-carvers so their skills could be shared, how to integrate the new Southern herbalists without overcrowding the healing corridors. Construction foremen sought approval for expansions. Elders from every lineage gathered to discuss rituals, naming ceremonies, and the blending of old songs with new melodies born here. I listened. I mediated. I'm blessed. I encouraged—my voice steady, my smile warm, even as my heart pulled relentlessly southward toward the pilgrims.

Secretly, in the quiet hours when the center slept, I prepared.

I packed a small satchel in the dim light of my chamber: dried provisions wrapped in waxed cloth, a fur-lined cloak against the high passes, a map marked with the most likely route Nathan would take to the Center. I spoke to trusted lieutenants—Talem among them—entrusting the day-to-day oversight. "I'll be gone no longer than necessary," I told them, voice low. "The gathering must continue, with or without me for a few days."

They nodded, eyes knowing. They had seen the shadow in my gaze, felt the urgency that radiated from me like heat from a forge. "We will hold the harmony," Talem said simply. "Go to your family. Bring them home."

Within a week, I decided. I would ride out—alone if needed—to meet Nathan, Tyler, and Souta on the path. I could not let the final miles pass without standing beside my husband. I could not let the boys face the shadow without their father's strength beside them. The thought of Nathan walking into that last confrontation alone was unbearable—a knife twisting slowly in my chest.

Reports from the Northern scouting groups arrived daily via swift riders and the occasional spiritual whisper carried on the wind. Two more small tribes had been found—scattered remnants of ancient lines, hidden in fjords and glacial valleys. The scouts had sung the old songs, shown the sigils, spoken of the Foreign Fire and the gathering. The tribes had wept, then packed. Now they were being escorted south, a slow but steady stream of fur-clad figures with sleds and dogs.

But the greater Northern Tribe—the main body—still waited.

Their messengers had come three times, bearing word of blockades: massive ice walls, unnatural and ancient, sealing the primary passes. "The winds will not move them," the messengers said, voices heavy. "They are bound by something older than winter. We feel the call, but the way is shut."

I had stared at the maps, fingers tracing the frozen routes until the parchment creased beneath my touch. I knew. Deep in my spirit I knew.

It would be Nathan.

In that final confrontation—when the shadow rose, when the Foreign Fire was unleashed in its fullest measure—God's power would break more than one enemy. The blast would ripple outward, across territories, across continents, melting ice, parting stone, shattering every barrier that kept the tribes from home. The North would feel it first: the great walls cracking, crumbling, dissolving into harmless snow. Then the others—the hidden valleys, the storm-locked islands, the forgotten mountains—would sense the release, the invitation, the triumph.

I believed it with every fiber of my being. I believed it because I believed in Nathan.

That night, as the center settled into quiet, I stood on the balcony of the central hall, overlooking the glowing rings of homes, the firelit squares, the people moving in harmony below. Three thousand five hundred lights flickered like stars brought to earth.

I lifted my face to the night sky, the wind cool against my cheeks.

"Soon," I whispered, voice breaking just a little. "Hold on, love. I'm coming."

Then I turned back inside to finish the preparations.

The gathering swelled. The harmony held. And the path south drew ever closer to its end.

(25) The Joining of the Threads

Gabriel's POV

By the evening of the fourth day since the East Wind pilgrims had set out, the tribal center had become a living archive of memory and miracle. The great central hall—now called the Hall of Union—glowed under the open sky, its mosaic walls catching the last rays of sunset like a thousand tiny flames. Tables stretched the length of the chamber, covered in every kind of record the scattered tribes had preserved through centuries of hiding: cracked leather journals, brittle papyrus scrolls, carved stone tablets, hand-stitched maps on deerskin, silk-wrapped scripts in languages half-forgotten, and bound logs of oral histories transcribed by trembling hands in hidden caves.

The joining began at dawn.

Groups formed naturally around the tables—scholars from the Western Wind, story-keepers from the South, rune-readers from the North, and the newly arrived Eastern elders who carried wind-carved wooden cylinders containing chants and genealogies. No one directed; the Spirit moved them. A woman from a lost Southern clan unrolled a faded map showing river routes long dried up; moments later, a Northern ice-scribe placed a matching fragment beside it, the lines aligning perfectly. Gaps that had haunted generations began to close.

One elder from the East Wind, a thin man with silver braids, lifted a small clay tablet etched with spiral sigils. "This speaks of a hidden valley where the West Wind Children sheltered during the great scattering," he said quietly. "We thought it myth."

A young woman from the Western contingent gasped, pulling forward a water-stained journal. "My great-grandmother wrote of the same valley. She said the river there never froze, even in the coldest years. Look—the coordinates match."

The hall filled with soft exclamations as pieces clicked into place: a missing branch of the lineage traced through a shared birthmark described in two separate logs; a forgotten migration path confirmed by overlapping star charts; the location of a sacred spring now revealed on three different maps. Tears fell freely. Laughter broke out when contradictions resolved into deeper truth—one account claiming a battle won by fire, another by wind, until a third scroll showed both occurring simultaneously, the elements dancing as one.

Meanwhile, more groups stepped forward from the growing crowd.

A family of seven—quiet, weathered, carrying only a single locked chest—approached the central platform. The father opened it with shaking hands. Inside lay a bundle of yellowed letters tied with red thread.

"We were the last keepers of the Ashen Line," he said, voice cracking. "Our people hid in the shadow of the smoking mountains. We have names—three hundred and twelve—that never reached the other Winds. We thought we were alone."

I placed a hand on the man's shoulder, feeling the tremor in him. "You are not alone anymore."

As the sun climbed, dreams and visions poured in like rain after drought. Spiritual leaders—prophets, seers, prayer warriors— gathered in a smaller circle beneath the open roof. One after another they spoke:

"I saw a frozen fjord break open at dawn, ships with white sails emerging." "A child with hair like flame stood on a cliff, calling the lost home." "Waters rose in the desert—clean, sweet, enough for thousands." "I heard singing from beneath the earth—voices of those still hidden."

I listened to every word, heart pounding. I wrote each vision in a fresh ledger, cross-referencing them with the maps and journals. Then I sent swift messengers—riders on swift horses and those gifted with the wind-whisper—to the proposed locations. "Go to the fjord of the white sails," I instructed. "Sing the old songs. Show the sigils. Tell them the gathering waits."

The land itself responded.

Where once there had been dry gullies, clear waterways now bubbled up—springs bursting from the earth as though uncapped by an unseen hand. Vegetation surged: tender green shoots pushed through cracked soil overnight, ripening into fruit-bearing vines within hours. Fields that had lain fallow for generations now waved with golden grain. Orchards bloomed out of season, heavy with figs and pomegranates. The people harvested with wonder, sharing freely—every basket filled to overflowing, yet never emptied.

I walked the new waterways at dusk, bare feet in the cool shallows. Fish darted beneath the surface—silver and fat, as though they too had been waiting. I knelt, cupped water in my hands, and drank. It tasted of life, of promise, of abundance prepared long before we arrived.

Everyone had a place.

The carpenter taught the weaver how to reinforce beams with living a vine. The healer showed the cook which herbs strengthened the blood. The child who dreamed visions was paired with an elder who wrote them down. The strong carried the weak; the wise listened to the simple.

No one stood idle. No one was overlooked. The empire was being rebuilt not by force, but by willing hearts moving as one.

As the sun dipped toward the horizon, casting long shadows across the Hall of Union, the sacred elders gathered in a tight circle at the center of the chamber. Their robes—woven from fibers of every Wind's heritage—brushed softly against one another, a tapestry of colors symbolizing the harmony they invoked. Incense burned low in clay bowls, sending spirals of fragrant smoke upward through the open roof, carrying their prayers to the heavens.

Elder Mara from the East Wind stepped forward first, her voice steady and resonant. "Brothers and sisters of the Spirit, the threads join. But our kin still wander in distant shadows. Let us summon them now—with heart and voice—as the Almighty draws them near."

The circle tightened. An elder from the North, his beard white as snow, raised his hands. "Lord of Winds and Flames, we call to the frozen fjords where the hidden clans shiver in isolation. Melt the ice of their doubt. Whisper through the blizzards: 'Come home.'"

A Southern seeress, eyes closed in vision, added her plea: "To the desert wanderers, parched and scattered, send dreams of flowing waters. Let them see the gathering fires. Draw them from the sands, O God—let them feel the pull of blood and promise."

From the West, Liora's voice rose like a wave: "For the island exiles, bound by false seas, break the chains anew. Send visions of unity, of the Center restored. Call them across the waters, that they may join the song."

The prayers wove together, voices overlapping in a sacred chorus: "To the mountains, the valleys, the forgotten plains—far and wide, across territories unseen—summon the lost. Let the earth itself cry out. Let the winds carry the invitation. Draw them, O Eternal One, into the harmony of Your people."

As they prayed, a gentle wind stirred within the hall—not from the open sky, but from within the circle itself. It rustled the scrolls on the tables, as if affirming the summons. Visions flashed among the elders: glimpses of distant figures stirring in sleep, rising with wide eyes, packing for journeys they could not yet explain.

I moved through the hall with purposeful strides, my presence a steady anchor amid the swelling activity. I paused at the storehouse entrance, where the keepers—strong-shouldered men and women with ledgers in hand—tallied the latest harvests.

"Storehouse men," I said, voice firm yet warm, "the land gives abundantly, but we must honor it. Keep detailed records of every crop stored: the bushels of grain from the new fields, the crates of figs and pomegranates, the barrels of dried fish from the Western arrivals. Note the dates of harvest, the quality, and the projected yield for the coming moons. Let nothing spoil through neglect. Our people grow; so must our provision."

One keeper, a broad man with ink-stained fingers, nodded solemnly. "As you say, Heir. We've begun a new ledger—every root, every seed accounted for. The waterways bring fresh hauls daily; we'll ensure the storehouses overflow without waste."

I clasped his forearm. "Good. The Almighty provides; we steward."

I continued to the construction yards, where hammers rang in rhythmic unison and saws whispered through blessed timber. The builders—sweaty, joyful, blending skills from every tribe— paused as I approached.

"Builders of the empire," I called, raising my voice above the din, "your hands shape our future. But remember: do not waste supplies. Every beam, every stone, every vine is a gift from the land. Measure twice, cut once. Reuse the scraps for smaller lodges or tools. Let harmony guide your work—no haste that breeds error, no excess that dishonors the provision."

A lead carpenter, her apron dusted with sawdust, wiped her brow and grinned. "We hear you, Gabriel. The vines grow as we weave them—living walls that strengthen with each day. No waste here; every piece finds its place, just as every person does."

Satisfied, I moved to the talliers—scribes and counters huddled over wide tables in a shaded pavilion, quills scratching ceaselessly.

"Talliers of the increase," I said, leaning over their ledgers, "your work is the backbone of our peace. Keep accurate records of every numerable thing: the rise in crops, the new tools forged, the livestock multiplying in the paddocks. And the people— every soul who arrives, every birth in the healing alcoves. Maintain the census diligently; let no name go unrecorded. Adhere to the districts—assign homes by lineage and need, ensuring balance across the rings."

The head census taker, an elderly woman with sharp eyes, dipped her quill and replied: "We do, Heir. The count stands at 3,512 this eve—twelve more from the Northern escorts. Districts are marked; no overcrowding, no isolation. The increase is tracked hourly; we see God's hand in every addition."

I exhaled, a quiet prayer of thanks on my lips. The empire was not just building—it was thriving, every role filled, every heart aligned.

As night fell, the summons continued in whispers and dreams, drawing the distant ones closer still. The threads were joining. The gaps were filling. And the final call was rising on every wind.

(26) Three Hearts, One Path

Tyler's POV

I don't know how long we've been walking. Days? Weeks? Time feels different now—like it's stretching thin, as a thread pulled too tight before it snaps. The path south is endless, cliffs on one side, crashing sea on the other, and every step makes my chest ache more. Haba is right in front of me, his white tunic catching the wind like a flag of surrender. Souta's hand is in mine, small and warm, squeezing every time the trail gets steep. He thinks I'm the strong one. He doesn't know I'm holding on to him, so I don't fall apart.

I keep replaying yesterday's talk on the outcrop. The way Haba's voice cracked when he said the price might be him. The way his tears fell into my hair. I've seen him bleed before—literal blood from battles—but this is worse. This is him preparing to leave us, and he's trying so hard to make it okay. He keeps smiling at us, keeps pointing out birds, keeps saying "We're almost there," as if he says it enough, the ending changes.

I hate that I'm angry at God. I know I shouldn't be. I know He's good. I've felt Him in visions, felt Him steady me when everything else spins. But right now it feels like He's asking too much. Why Haba? Why not someone else? Why not me? I'd trade places in a heartbeat if it meant he could stay. Dad would hate hearing that. He'd probably grab me by the shoulders and tell me I'm enough, that I don't have to carry everything. But Dad's not here. Dad's back at the center, building homes and holding the tribe together while we walk toward something I can't even picture without crying.

Souta tugs my hand. "Tyler? You're squeezing too hard."

I loosen my grip. "Sorry."

He looks up at me with those big, trusting eyes. "Are you thinking about the bad thing again?"

I swallow. "Yeah."

He nods like he understands, even though he's only nine. "Me too. But Haba said God wins. So… maybe it won't be as bad as we think."

I want to believe him. I want to be the big brother he needs. But every time I look at Haba's back, I see the shadow behind him growing. Not a real shadow—something worse. Something hungry. I've glimpsed it in flashes: a figure made of smoke and broken promises, eyes like coals, reaching for Haba like he's the last light it can snuff out. I haven't told anyone. Not yet. I'm scared that if I say it out loud, it becomes more real.

Last night, when we camped in a sheltered cove, I couldn't sleep. Haba was sitting by the fire, staring into the flames like they were telling him secrets. I crawled over, wrapped my arms around him from behind, and just held on. He didn't say anything at first. Then he covered my hands with his and whispered, "I'm so proud of you, Tyler. You're going to be more than I ever was."

I cried into his back until my shirt was soaked. He let me. He didn't try to fix it. He just let me feel the hurt. That's what makes it worse—he's so gentle about leaving. Like he's already saying goodbye in every touch.

I don't want to be brave anymore. I just want my Haba.

But the path keeps going. And so do we.

Souta's POV

The sea is loud today. It roars like it's angry, like it knows something we don't. I hold Tyler's hand so tight my fingers hurt, but I don't let go. Tyler is tall and strong, and he smells like salt and Haba's tunic. Haba walks ahead, and every time he looks back to check on us, he smiles. But his smile is different now. It's softer. Like it hurts to make it.

I keep thinking about my mom and dad. They went out in a little boat when the storm came. They said they'd be back before dark. They weren't. Mara found me in the cave afterward, crying so hard I couldn't breathe. She said, "The wind took them, but it left you." I didn't understand then. I think I do now.

Haba is going to be taken too. Not by wind. By something bigger. Something dark. I felt it when the mark on my arm got hot last night—like it was warning me. The flame inside the circle burned bright, then dimmed, then burned again. Like it was breathing with me. Scared like me.

I don't want to be scared alone.

Tyler's quiet today. He keeps looking at Haba like he's memorizing him. I do that too. I watch the way Haba's hair moves in the wind. The way his hands are gentle when he helps someone over a rock. The way he hums old songs when he thinks no one's listening. I want to remember everything. If he goes away, I want to keep him inside me like a treasure.

Yesterday, he let me ride on his shoulders for a while. My legs were tired, and he just scooped me up without asking. From up there I could see the whole line of people—elders, warriors, children—all following him. Like he's the leader even when he's not trying to be. I leaned down and whispered in his ear, "You're the best Haba ever."

He laughed, but it sounded wet. "You're the best Keeper ever, little one."

I don't feel like the best anything. I just feel small. But when I'm with them—Tyler holding my hand, Haba carrying me—I feel bigger. Like maybe I can be brave enough for both of us.

Last night I dreamed of the Center. It was huge—tall stone towers touching clouds, gardens everywhere, people singing. Haba was there, but he was glowing so bright I could barely look. Then the shadow came. Big. Angry. It tried to swallow him. He raised his hand, and light exploded—brighter than the sun. The shadow screamed and disappeared. When the light faded… Haba was gone. Just empty air where he stood.

I woke up crying. Tyler was already awake. He pulled me close and said, "It's okay. It was just a dream."

But it didn't feel like just a dream. It felt like a warning.

I look at Haba now. He's helping an elderly woman over a slippery stone. His face is tired, but kind. I want to run up and hug him forever. I want to tell him not to go. I want to tell him I love him more than the cliffs, more than the wind song, more than anything.

But I don't say it.

Because if I say it, it might make the goodbye come faster.

So I just hold Tyler's hand tighter.

And keep walking.

Nathan's Preliminary Visions

The fire in the cove had burned low, its embers glowing like scattered stars against the black sand. The camp slept pilgrims wrapped in blankets, children curled against parents, the soft rhythm of waves providing a lullaby. Only Nathan remained awake, back against the boulder, knees drawn up, tears still drying on his cheeks from the visions that had come like a relentless tide.

The first vision had shown the completed gathering: tribes streaming into the valley, Tyler and Souta standing on the high platform, Gabriel at the base with arms wide, the empire reborn in light. The second had shown the shadow rising, Nathan standing alone, the final unleashing of the Foreign Fire, and then… silence. Nothingness. No trace. Only warmth lingering on the stones. The third had been gentler: Nathan stepping into light, looking back once at his family waving below, then turning forward into home.

He wiped his face with the back of his hand, exhaling shakily. The weight was no longer hidden. It pressed against his ribs, heavy and certain.

A soft footfall broke the quiet. Mara approached, her silver braids catching the ember-glow. She carried no lantern; the night itself seemed to part for her. She settled beside him on the sand, close enough that their shoulders nearly touched.

"You saw it all," she said quietly. Not a question.

Nathan nodded. "Every step. The reunion. The shadow. The price."

Mara's gaze remained on the dying fire. "And you will walk it."

"I will."

She exhaled slowly. "Then the time has come to divide the path. The pilgrims must continue to the gathering place where Gabriel waits. But you—" She turned to him, eyes steady. "You and the boys must go to the Central Tribe. The heart that has been hidden. The scroll from Souta's cave makes it clear: only when the Keeper's flame joins the Central Flame will the final door open. That path lies slightly west of the main route—through the narrow pass of the Whispering Peaks. The pilgrims cannot follow. The wards will not permit it."

Nathan's throat tightened. "And you will lead them the rest of the way?"

Mara placed a weathered hand on his forearm. "I will. The East Wind has guarded thresholds for generations. I know the songs that calm the land, the signs that guide safe passage. The pilgrims will reach Gabriel unharmed. I swear it on the wind itself."

Nathan looked toward the sleeping boys—Tyler curled protectively around Souta, Souta's small hand clutching Tyler's tunic even in sleep. "They'll want to stay with the others. They'll fight me on this."

"They will," Mara agreed. "But they will also follow you. You are their Haba. And they sense what is coming, even if they do not yet name it."

Silence stretched between them, broken only by the waves.

"When?" Nathan asked.

"At first light," Mara replied. "Before the camp wakes fully. A clean break is kinder."

Nathan closed his eyes. "Then I need to speak to Gabriel. One last time."

He reached inward, finding the familiar thread of connection that had bound them since the estate days. The link flared warm and immediate, as though Gabriel had been waiting.

Love, Gabriel's voice came through, raw and urgent. *You're still awake.*

Always, Nathan sent back, trying for lightness. *I saw the end tonight. All of it.*

A pause. Then, softer: *Tell me.*

Nathan poured the visions through the link—images of the gathering, the shadow, the light, the silence. He held nothing back.

When the last image faded, Gabriel's thought came like a held breath. *You're going to the Central Tribe. Alone with the boys.*

Not alone. With them. But yes… the pilgrims must take the eastern road to you. Mara will lead them.

Another silence, longer this time. Nathan could almost see Gabriel standing on the balcony of the central hall, looking south, fists clenched on the stone railing.

Then I'm coming to you, Gabriel finally sent. *I'm leaving tonight. I'll fly. I might not make it in time—I know that—but I have to try. I won't let you face this without me.*

Nathan's heart cracked open. *Gabe… the gathering needs you here. The people need you.*

The people need their family whole, Gabriel countered fiercely. *Tyler and Souta need their father. And I need you. Even if it's only for the last miles. Even if it's only to hold you one more time before… before whatever comes.*

Tears slipped down Nathan's face again. *You'll break their hearts if you leave them leaderless.*

I've already spoken to Talem and the elders. They know what's coming. They'll hold the center until we return. Or until… His thought faltered, then steadied. *I'm coming, Nathan. No argument. I love you. I'm on my way.*

The link pulsed once—warm, fierce, final—then quieted.

Nathan opened his eyes. Mara was watching him, understanding in her gaze.

"He's coming," Nathan whispered.

Mara nodded once. "Then we move at dawn. Let the boys sleep a little longer. They'll need their strength."

<hr>

The camp stirred slowly. Pilgrims rose, folded blankets, packed provisions. Mara moved among them with quiet authority, giving instructions in the old tongue. The pilgrims accepted her leadership without question; the East Wind had earned their trust on the long road from the cliffs.

Nathan knelt beside the sleeping boys. He brushed Tyler's hair back, then Souta's. Both stirred, blinking up at him in the pale dawn.

"Haba?" Tyler mumbled, voice thick with sleep.

Nathan smiled, though it cost him. "We need to talk, sweethearts. Come with me."

He led them a short distance from the camp to a sheltered outcrop overlooking the sea. Mara waited there, staff in hand, the pilgrims gathering behind her at a respectful distance.

Tyler's eyes narrowed as he took in the scene. "What's happening?"

Nathan knelt so he was eye-level with them. "The path divides here. The pilgrims must continue east to the gathering place where Gabriel waits. Mara will lead them. They'll be safe. They'll be home soon."

Souta's small face crumpled. "But... we're going with them, right?"

Nathan shook his head gently. "No, little Keeper. You and Tyler and I... we have to go west. To the Central Tribe. The heart that's

199

been hidden all this time. The scroll showed us the way. Only when your flame joins the Central Flame will the final gathering be complete.”

Tyler’s jaw tightened. “You’re sending us away from everyone else. From Dad. From safety.”

“Not away,” Nathan said softly. “Forward. To finish what we started.”

Souta’s eyes filled. “But I don’t want to leave Mara. Or the others. Or… or the wind song.”

Nathan pulled them both into his arms. “I know. I know it hurts. But this is the path God has set. And He’s never led us wrong.”

Tyler buried his face in Nathan’s shoulder, voice muffled. “Dad’s coming, isn’t he? I can feel it. He’s… he’s flying to us.”

Nathan’s breath caught. “Yes. He’s coming. But he might not reach us before… before the end. And if he doesn’t…” He swallowed hard. “Then we carry on. The three of us. Until the very last step.”

Souta clung tighter. “Promise you won’t leave us alone.”

“I promise I’ll be with you every heartbeat,” Nathan whispered. “Even when you can’t see me.”

Mara stepped forward, placing a gentle hand on each boy’s head. “I will bring your people safely to Gabriel. You have my word. Now go. The Whispering Peaks wait.”

Nathan rose, taking the boys’ hands. He looked back once at the pilgrims’ faces he had come to love, hands raised in blessing and farewell.

Then he turned west.

Behind him, Mara lifted her staff. The pilgrims began to move eastward, voices rising in the old traveling song.

Ahead, the narrow pass of the Whispering Peaks opened like a doorway carved by time itself.

Nathan, Tyler, and Souta stepped through—three hearts bound by love, faith, and the knowledge that the final miles would test them all.

Somewhere far to the north, Gabriel launched into the sky, wings of force unfurling behind him, eyes fixed on the southern horizon.

He flew with everything he had.

Hoping against hope that he would be in time.

(27) The Awakening of the Central Tribe

The trio crested the final ridge at dawn on the fifth day, the air thin and sharp with the scent of pine and ancient stone. Below them lay a vast, bowl-shaped valley cradled by snow-dusted peaks—untouched, timeless, as though the earth itself had folded it away from the world for millennia.

Nathan halted first, breath catching in his throat. Tyler and Souta pressed close on either side, their small hands finding his without a word. The valley shimmered in the morning light: towering stone spires carved with spiraling sigils that matched the maps from Souta's scroll, wide plazas ringed by stepped terraces blooming with unexpected greenery, and at the heart—a massive circular temple of white marble, its dome open to the sky like a cupped hand reaching for heaven.

This was no ruin. Smoke curled from chimneys in orderly clusters of dwellings. Figures moved between buildings—men in long robes of deep indigo, women carrying baskets of fresh grain, children chasing one another across flagstone paths. The Central Tribe had not been lost; it had been waiting.

Souta placed a trembling small hand on Nathan's arm. "The legends spoke of them swallowed by the mountains," he whispered, voice thick. "Not destroyed. Hidden. Preserved."

A low horn sounded from the valley floor—three long, resonant notes that vibrated through the stone under their feet. The people below froze, then turned as one toward the ridge. A murmur rose, swelling into a chant in the old tongue, words that Nathan recognized from the cavern scrolls: *The Foreign Fire has come. The Keeper walks. The gathering begins.*

Nathan felt the pull in his chest—the same inexorable draw that had guided him through every Wind. He lifted his hand, palm open, and light flared softly from his skin, answering the horn like a beacon.

From the temple steps emerged a delegation: an elder woman with silver hair braided with feathers, flanked by warriors in armor etched with flame motifs, and—most strikingly—a boy no older than twelve, bearing a staff topped with a living flame that danced without consuming the wood. The mark on his forearm mirrored Souta's, but larger, brighter, pulsing in rhythm with the younger boy's.

The elder woman raised her staff. "We are the Children of the Center," she called, voice carrying clear across the valley. "We have guarded the heart since the great scattering. Our fathers spoke of the day the scattered Winds would return, led by the Foreign Fire and the Keeper's flame. We have waited. And now we see."

Nathan descended the path first, the boys at his heels. As he reached the valley floor, the elder woman stepped forward and placed her hands on his shoulders. Her eyes—deep brown, ancient—searched his.

"You are the one the visions named," she said softly. "The man who carries fire not his own. The one who will pay the final price to open the way."

Nathan nodded once, throat tight. "I am Nathan. And these are my sons—Tyler, bearer of visions, and Souta, the Keeper whose mark has awakened."

The woman turned to Souta. The boy's flame-mark flared in response to the staff-bearer's. She knelt, cupping his face gently. "Little brother," she murmured. "Your light has called us awake.

The Central Flame has slumbered since the days of captivity. It waited for you."

Souta swallowed, eyes wide. "I... I didn't know what it meant. I just followed the pull."

The elder smiled, tears shining. "That is enough. The pure heart needs no greater knowledge."

She rose and gestured toward the temple. "Come. The Central Tribe has prepared a place for you. Our halls are open. Our stores are full. The land has kept us hidden, but it has also kept us ready. The prophecies spoke of this day—the reunion of all Winds under one fire."

As they walked through the streets, Nathan saw the evidence of preservation: granaries carved into living rock, still stocked with grain from seasons long past yet miraculously unspoiled; springs bubbling pure and clear, channels directing water to every dwelling; orchards heavy with fruit that should have taken decades to mature. The Central Tribe had lived in harmony with the land, guided by visions and ancient wards that kept the world at bay.

In the great temple hall, a massive stone table stood at the center, etched with a map of the four Winds converging on this very valley. Elders from each group arrived—Western sea-bearers, Southern vine-weavers, Northern ice-keepers—each placing a relic on the table: a shell, a woven cord, a carved ice shard, a wind-flute. When Souta laid his small scroll beside them, the flame on his arm and the staff-bearers joined in a single, steady glow, illuminating the map. Lines of light traced between the Winds, meeting at the temple.

The elder woman spoke again, voice ringing. "The heart has been found. The body is complete. But the final breath—the final gathering—awaits the Foreign Fire's last act."

Nathan felt the weight settle more heavily. The shadow he had sensed for weeks was closer now, stirring in the valley's depths like a storm gathering beyond the peaks. He looked at Tyler and Souta—their faces alight with wonder yet shadowed by the knowledge he had shared on the path.

Tyler stepped forward, voice steady despite the tremor in it. "We came to bring everyone home. And we will. Whatever it costs."

Souta nodded, small hand slipping into Tyler's. "Together."

The elder woman placed her hands on both boys' shoulders. "Then let the feast begin. Tonight, we celebrate the awakening. Tomorrow... we prepare for the final call."

As the sun climbed higher, drums rose from every corner of the valley—deep, joyful rhythms that echoed off the mountains. Tables groaned under fresh bread, roasted meats, and fruits bursting with sweetness. Voices lifted in song, old and new blending as one.

Nathan stood at the temple steps, watching his sons laugh with the Central children, the flames on their arms flickering in harmony. For a moment, the shadow receded. Peace held.

But he knew it was the calm before the final storm.

And when it broke, the gathering would be complete—every tribe, every heart, drawn home.

Even as one light prepared to step into the greater light beyond.

(28) The Final Shadow

The valley of the Central Tribe lay shrouded in an unnatural stillness as the first hints of dawn crept over the mountain ridges. A dense, eerie fog had exploded into the basin overnight thick and swirling, like the breath of some ancient entity stirring from slumber. It clung to the stone spires and draped the terraced plazas in a veil of milky white, muffling sounds and blurring edges until the world felt like a dream on the verge of shattering. No birds sang. No wind whispered through the sigil-carved towers. The air hung heavy, pregnant with unspoken finality.

Only Nathan was awake.

He moved through the street segments like a ghost in his white tunic, footsteps silent on the flagstones worn smooth by centuries of hidden feet. The fog parted reluctantly before him, closing behind like a curtain drawn on a stage he could no longer leave. Tyler and Souta slept in the guest chamber of the temple, exhausted from the feast and the revelations of the day before. The Central elders rested in their dwellings, unaware of the hour's weight. Even the flames in the eternal braziers burned low, as if holding their breath.

Nathan's heart pounded with a rhythm that echoed his prayers—fervent, unyielding, laced with the quiet desperation of a man who knew his time was measured in heartbeats. He walked the winding paths, hands clasped before him, eyes lifted to the obscured sky.

"Holy Spirit," he whispered, voice trembling yet resolute, "descend upon me now. Fill this valley with Your peace. Calm the storm within my soul, that I may stand unshaken in the face of what comes. Let Your comfort wrap around Tyler and Souta, around Gabriel racing toward us, around every scattered heart You've called home."

He paused at a low stone wall, fingers tracing the etched sigils that pulsed faintly under his touch. The fog swirled thicker here, carrying a chill that seeped into his bones.

"Father God," he continued, voice rising slightly, "grant me strength beyond my own. You who parted seas and shattered chains, arm me now for this final battle. Let Your power flow through me like rivers of living water. I am Your vessel—broken, willing, ready."

His breath fogged the air, mingling with the mist. He walked on, entering the lush gardens at the city's heart—terraces blooming with night-blooming flowers that glowed softly in the gloom, their petals unfurling as if in silent worship.

"Jesus, my Lord," Nathan prayed, kneeling on the dew-slick grass, face turned upward, "lay Your hand over me. As You cast out legions with a word, empower me to banish this final demon—the oppressor of not one soul, but many. It has tormented the tribes, twisted hearts, sown shadows across generations. In Your name, I will stand against it. Protect my sons. Protect my husband. Let this victory echo through eternity."

For the first hour, he remained there praying without ceasing, words flowing into tears, tears into silence, silence into a deep, holy resolve. The fog seemed to listen, swirling closer, as if the valley itself absorbed his supplications. Strength built within him, a warm current against the cold, divine assurance threading through his veins.

Then, from the shadows beyond the garden's edge—where ancient graves lay carved into the valley walls—a figure emerged.

The old man.

He stepped from the mist like a specter unearthed, his form gaunt and twisted, eyes burning with malevolent fire. This was the tormentor who had shadowed Nathan since the islands—the embodiment of denied mercy, rejected light, the bitterness that had festered into something monstrous. His presence reeked of decay, of graves long sealed.

Nathan rose slowly, standing firm as the man approached. The fog coiled around the intruder's feet, as if recoiling from his touch.

"You think your prayers change anything, Foreign Fire?" the old man hissed, voice like gravel scraping bone. "Look at you— alone in the mist, whispering to a God who demands your life as payment. Your boys will wake to an empty world. Your husband will arrive to ashes. The tribes you've gathered? They'll scatter again, broken by the shadow you can't defeat. You're no Moses. You're a fool chasing glory into the grave."

Dreaded words poured forth, laced with venom—visions of Tyler sobbing alone, Souta lost in darkness, Gabriel crumbling under grief. They clawed at Nathan's mind, seeking cracks in his resolve.

But Nathan stood firm. "In the name of Jesus Christ," he declared, voice steady, "your lies hold no power here."

The old man snarled, features contorting into something inhuman. He lunged—clawed hands outstretched, body propelled by unnatural speed, aiming for Nathan's throat.

In that frozen instant, light exploded from the fog.

Two angels materialized—tall, radiant, armored in gleaming silver that cut through the mist like dawn's first rays. Their wings unfurled with a sound like thunder muffled by clouds, and they grasped the old man mid-leap, freezing him in place. His body went rigid, suspended inches from Nathan, eyes wide with rage and sudden terror.

The angels' bright appearances held for a heartbeat—faces serene, eyes blazing with holy fire. Then, a shift: shadows writhed up from the ground, coiling around the old man like chains. Two devils overtook him—dark forms with eyes like smoldering coals, forms twisting in glee as they latched onto his limbs. The angels released their hold and stepped back, standing resolute beside Nathan, their light undimmed.

The old man convulsed, a guttural scream tearing from his throat. "No! Not yet!"

Under the orders of the Almighty, the devils dragged him downward. The ground parted—not with earthquake or violence, but with a silent unraveling, revealing a yawning void that pulsed with infernal heat. The man—tormentor, oppressor, vessel of the final demon—thrashed futilely as he was pulled into the underverse. His screams echoed briefly, then were silenced as the earth sealed over him.

He had died. His soul consigned to Hades, the oppressor banished to the realm of the damned.

The fog thinned slightly, as if the valley exhaled in relief.

The holy angels turned to Nathan, their presence a balm against the lingering chill. One placed a luminous hand on his shoulder, warmth spreading through him like sunlight after storm.

"Press on, faithful one," the angel said, voice resonant and kind. "Your time is at hand. The shadow of the Central Tribe awaits—the entity that has guarded this valley in darkness, feeding on the hidden years. It is your greatest challenge to date, for it embodies the collective wounds of the scattered: isolation, forgotten promises, the ache of exile."

The second angel nodded, eyes shining. "But you do not face it alone. Call on the power of God, as you have prayed. Wield the Foreign Fire without restraint. Victory is assured—not by your strength, but by His. And remember though your path diverges, love endures. Your family will carry the light you ignite."

Nathan bowed his head, tears of awe and resolve mingling on his cheeks. "Thank You," he whispered. "For the strength. For the peace. For the hand over me."

The angels inclined their heads in reverence, then dissolved into the lifting fog—fading like stars at dawn, leaving behind a faint glow that lingered in the air.

Nathan stood alone once more but fortified. The gardens bloomed brighter around him, flowers unfurling as if in witness. The fog began to dissipate, revealing the first true rays of morning sun.

His greatest challenge lay ahead—the shadow entity, vast and ancient, coiled at the valley's core.

But so did his God.

With a final prayer on his lips, Nathan turned back toward the temple.

The boys would wake soon.

Gabriel flew closer with every heartbeat.

And the final battle called.

(29) The Shadow and the Flame

The fog had lifted by full morning, but the valley felt heavier for it—as though the air itself remembered the night's confrontation and now waited in tense anticipation. Sunlight poured golden over the stone spires and terraced gardens, catching on the sigils carved into every surface, making them shimmer like veins of living light. Yet beneath the beauty lay a growing pressure, a low vibration that thrummed through the flagstones and into Nathan's bones.

He had returned to the temple steps just as Tyler and Souta woke. They found him there, sitting with hands open on his knees, face lifted to the sky, still praying in soft undertones. The boys approached quietly, sensing the shift in him the way children sense storms before the first drop falls.

"Haba?" Tyler whispered, voice small.

Nathan opened his eyes and smiled—tender, tired, complete. "I'm here, sweethearts."

Souta climbed onto the step beside him, pressing close. "Something's different. The air feels… big. Like it's holding its breath."

Nathan drew them both into his arms, one on each side. "It is. The shadow is rising. The entity the angels spoke of—it's been here longer than any of us. Feeding on the hidden years, on the loneliness of waiting, on every unhealed wound the tribes carried. It thinks this valley belongs to it now. But it doesn't. This place was made for light."

Tyler swallowed hard. "You're going to fight it. Alone."

"Not alone," Nathan said firmly. "God fights with me. And you two—you carry the Keeper's flame and the visions. You'll stand where I need you to stand. But first..." He looked toward the central plaza, where the elders were beginning to gather, drawn by the same unspoken pull. "First we gather the people. They deserve to know what's coming."

Word spread quickly. By mid-morning, the entire Central Tribe—joined by the pilgrims who had arrived during the night—filled the great circular plaza. Thousands stood in reverent silence, faces turned toward the temple steps where Nathan, Tyler, and Souta waited. Mara stood at the front, staff planted like an anchor. The boy with the living-flame staff stood beside her, eyes wide.

Nathan stepped forward. His voice carried without effort, amplified not by magic but by the authority that rested on him.

"Brothers and sisters of the Central Tribe, of every Wind—today the gathering reaches its fullness. But before the empire can rise completely, one last shadow must fall. An entity has claimed this valley in darkness, twisting the very promise of home into isolation and despair. It is ancient, powerful, and it fears the light we bring. Today, in the name of the Almighty, I will face it."

A murmur rippled through the crowd—fear, awe, resolve.

Tyler stepped up beside him, voice steady despite the tremor in his hands. "We've seen the visions. We've felt the call. Haba isn't fighting for himself. He's fighting for all of us—for every heart that waited, for every child who will be born here free."

Souta lifted his arm. The flame-mark blazed bright, golden, and unwavering. "And this… this is the sign. The Keeper's flame joins the Central Flame. The door opens today."

The elders bowed their heads. Some wept openly. Others lifted hands in silent prayer.

Nathan looked at the boys one last time—memorizing their faces, the way sunlight caught in Tyler's curls, the way Souta's small fingers curled around the edge of his tunic.

"I love you both," he said softly. "More than words can carry. Whatever happens next—know that I go willingly, because love demands it. And because God is faithful."

He kissed each forehead, lingering, breathing them in.

 The three boys—Tyler, Souta, and the Central boy whose flame-mark mirrored Souta's—stood close behind him, their faces pale but resolute. The gathered thousands watched from the plaza's edge, breath held, prayers already murmuring like a distant tide.

Nathan turned to them first.

"Souta," he said softly, voice steady despite the ache in his chest, "stand on the symbol stone of your fire."

The small Keeper walked forward without hesitation. His feet found the etched circle where a golden flame spiraled eternally. The moment he stood upon it, the mark on his arm blazed bright, answering like a heartbeat.

"Tyler," Nathan continued, "stand on the leadership stone of your calling."

Tyler moved to the second stone—carved with the sigil of an open hand crowned by light. He planted his feet firmly, shoulders squared, though his hands trembled at his sides.

The Central boy, eyes shining with quiet awe, took the third stone—the twin flame symbol beside Souta's. The three markings ignited in unison, a golden chord that thrummed through the ground, vibrating up through Nathan's bones.

Nathan stepped onto the fourth stone at the center—the Foreign Fire sigil, a blazing star encircled by thorns. The instant his foot touched it, the door responded.

An ancient *pop* echoed—sharp, final, like the snap of a lock forged in eternity. A sudden pump of thick mist erupted from every seam, flooding the basin in a choking white cloud that swallowed light and sound. The slabs groaned once, then cracked. Stone crumbled inward with a low, grinding roar, dust and fragments cascading into the black void below. A deepened gasp rose from the depths—cold, hungry, ancient, as though the earth itself had exhaled after holding its breath for millennia.

The mist cleared just enough to reveal the yawning staircase descending into shadow.

Nathan turned to the boys.

His voice was gentle, but there was no room for argument.

"Get yourselves to the head elder. Now. Go."

Souta's eyes filled instantly. "Haba—"

Tyler's jaw clenched, tears already brimming. "We're not leaving you—"

Nathan cupped their faces, one in each hand, thumbs brushing their cheeks. "You are. This is the path. You carry the flame and the vision—you've done what was asked. Now go. Be safe. Be ready. I love you both more than anything in this world or the next."

He kissed their foreheads—first Tyler, then Souta—lingering long enough to breathe them in, to memorize the warmth of their skin, the scent of their hair. Then he released them.

The boys hesitated only a heartbeat longer before turning and running up the steps toward the waiting elders, tears streaming, voices choked with sobs.

Nathan faced the distant crowd—thousands strong, every face turned toward him.

He raised his arms.

His voice thundered across the valley—not with volume alone, but with heavenly authority that carried like rolling thunder wrapped in grace:

"Pray! Hold your ground where you stand! Do not move from your place. Do not fear. Lift your voices to the Almighty for deliverance. He goes before us. He is with us. Pray!"

A wave of prayer rose immediately low at first, then swelling into a mighty chorus. Elders dropped to their knees. Warriors clasped hands. Children joined the old songs. The line tightened, a living wall of faith and intercession stretching around the basin's rim.

Nathan turned back to the broken doorway.

He drew a deep breath.

Then he descended the steps into the depths of the shadow.

For the first two stories down, darkness swallowed everything. He could see only the two steps in front of him—then nothing. The air grew colder, heavier, pressing against his chest like a living weight. Fear whispered at the edges of his mind, soft and insidious. It told him he was not loved, that his presence was a waste of human flesh, and his life was meaningless. Your god is surely leading you to your doom and he does not care about your family. What is your family, another man and a child? You are not the holy man you think you are.

Then the Holy Spirit came—soft, warm, overwhelming. Peace flooded him like a river breaking through drought. *"You are the son of the Great I AM. God is your refuge, a strong tower, a friend that sticks closer than a brother. He is your all in all. In Him you will find your rest, your peace, and your reassurance. God has called you from the ashes and claimed you as His own. You are of a royal priesthood. God has ordained you to carry His banner before the time of war. He will gird you with the tools you need."* Nathan exhaled, shoulders easing. He took the next step. And the next. Faith steps into the black.

As Nathan plunged deeper into the abyss, the shadow's malevolence thickened into a palpable, sentient force—a choking miasma that clawed at his lungs, squeezed his soul, and whispered insidious doubts into the recesses of his mind. It was no mere darkness; it was alive, ancient, a primordial hatred born from the void before creation, seeking to extinguish the spark of divinity within him. His chest heaved, every breath a battle, every thought a fragile flame flickering against an encroaching gale.

But in that suffocating grip, Nathan's spirit ignited. He parted his lips, and from the depths of his being erupted the eternal Word, a lifeline forged in faith.

"The Lord is my shepherd; I shall not want," he intoned, his voice a tremor at first, raw with vulnerability, laced with the ache of a man who had lost everything yet clung to hope. "Yea, though I walk through the valley of the shadow of death, I will fear no evil: for Thou art with me; Thy rod and Thy staff, they comfort me…"

The words swelled, gaining momentum like a river breaking a dam, echoing off the jagged, unseen walls with a resonance that shook the foundations of the pit. Each syllable was a thunderclap of defiance, a beacon piercing the gloom.

"No weapon formed against me shall prosper… I put on the whole armor of God… having done all, to stand… the righteous stand firm…"

Scripture after scripture exploded outward, not as rote recitation, but as living fire—searing truths that rent the fog of despair, illuminating the path with flashes of celestial clarity. The darkness recoiled like a wounded beast, shrieking in agony as fissures of light cracked its impenetrable veil.

"God, please send me the armor to fight this demon. I ask for the holy angels to descend and arm me in this moment. The time is at hand." Nathan's voice echoed loudly and distinctively.

Then, in a cataclysmic surge, heavenly radiance erupted from every crevice, a torrent of pure, blinding glory that flooded the cavern with the unfiltered essence of God's realm. It was a light that burned away illusion, revealing the raw beauty and terror of the divine—warm as a father's embrace, fierce as a warrior's gaze. Archangels descended in majestic formations, their wings ablaze with ethereal fire, swords unsheathed and humming with power, their very presence charging the air with electric holiness, making every molecule vibrate in worship.

From the surface above, the pit's orifice blazed like a supernova, forcing the Central Tribe to avert their eyes, tears streaming down weathered faces. The elders' voices rose above the deafening roar of communal prayer, hoarse with fervor and unyielding resolve:

"Hold rank! Continue in prayer! God is moving—He is here among us! He is shielding and helping Nathan below to prepare! We can do no less!"

The prayer line constricted like a heartbeat, hands interlocking in unbreakable bonds, voices merging into a symphony of supplication—a human bulwark fortified by divine grace, where fear dissolved into unbreakable unity.

Below, the celestial host encircled Nathan, their auras weaving a tapestry of protection and empowerment. One archangel, eyes like molten gold, girded him with the belt of truth, its leather humming with unassailable integrity. Another fastened the breastplate of righteousness, cool metal fusing to his skin like a second heart, pulsing with moral fortitude. A third slipped the shoes of the gospel of peace onto his feet, grounding him in serenity amid chaos. The fourth raised the shield of faith—impenetrable, shimmering—and crowned him with the helmet of salvation, its weight a comforting reminder of redemption's cost.

Arrows of incandescent light etched themselves into the armor, divine inscriptions from the hand of the Almighty, each one a promise etched in eternity: strength in weakness, victory in surrender.

"March on," the angels intoned in unison, their voices a harmonious blend of thunderous command and tender compassion, reverberating through Nathan's bones like the very breath of creation. "The victory is the Lord's—and it flows through you."

Nathan's form ignited with an inner conflagration, white fire coursing through his veins, radiating outward in waves of purifying heat. He advanced with purposeful strides, God's army trailing in his wake, archangels flanking him like eternal guardians. The heavenly host illuminated the depths like a constellation of living stars, banishing shadows that had festered for eons, revealing hidden horrors that withered under the gaze of holiness.

The earth trembled violently, a guttural quake that mirrored the turmoil in Nathan's soul—the weight of destiny, the sting of sacrifice, the exhilaration of purpose.

Before him, the entity materialized in all its grotesque majesty, a colossus that warped perception itself: a writhing mixture of inky shadows and razor-edged bone, its form shifting like nightmares given flesh. It exhaled plumes of sulfurous flame, each breath a gale of decay that carried the screams of lost souls, the acrid stench of forgotten sins. Its eyes—abyssal voids—sucked in light, promising oblivion, stirring in Nathan a primal terror that clashed with his unyielding faith.

Yet he stood resolute, feet planted like ancient oaks, as a sword of ethereal flame materialized in his grip—its blade alive with the fire of judgment, hilt warm with the touch of grace.

The final battle ignited, a clash of worlds where heaven stormed the gates of hell.

"In the name of Jesus Christ," Nathan proclaimed, his voice cracking with raw emotion—love for the lost, grief for the broken, fury at the deceiver—"I call down the holy fire of God!"

Reality tore asunder overhead, a rift in space and time birthing a colossal pillar of divine luminescence, brighter than a galaxy's core, slamming into the entity with the force of colliding worlds. The beast staggered, its colossal frame crumpling against the cavern wall, a bellow of pain echoing like the death throes of empires.

Undeterred, Nathan surged forward, one giant leap in flight, heart pounding with a fusion of adrenaline and divine ecstasy, swinging the flaming sword in a sweeping arc, cleaving through the creature's visage with a sizzle of seared shadow-flesh. Black ichor erupted in foul torrents, evaporating against the stone in hisses of defeat. Empowered by supernatural might, he seized the monstrosity by its throat—fingers vise-like, infused with the strength of legions—and hoisted it aloft, muscles straining yet unbreakable.

The entity writhed in futile rage, its roars a symphony of despair, but Nathan ascended—propelled by muscled wings unseen, bursting through the earth's crust in a geyser of rock and light, far from the pit's sunken maw. They spiraled into the open sky, toward the jagged embrace of the nearest mountain ridge, the wind whipping Nathan's hair, carrying the scent of freedom and impending triumph.

At that precise instant, Gabriel touched down near the temple steps, his landing a seismic thud that buckled the ground. His wings of radiant force folded inward, vanishing in a shimmer. Tyler and Souta hurled themselves at him, small arms wrapping around his legs in desperate relief, their sobs mingling with joy. Gabriel's face contorted in a storm of emotions—horror at the peril, awe at the miracle—as he gazed upward, witnessing Nathan and the thrashing abomination locked in aerial combat.

"Love..." he whispered, his voice fracturing like glass under pressure, tears carving paths down his cheeks—love for his brother, for humanity, for the God who orchestrated it all.

High in the firmament, Nathan uttered the climactic decree, his words infused with the weight of prophecy fulfilled.

"In the name of the Father, the Son, and the Holy Spirit—I command evil be eternally destroyed!"

A cataclysm of a thousand thunderclaps rent the heavens, the air itself fracturing under the assault. Light exploded from Nathan's core—brighter than a billion suns igniting at once, a supernova of sanctity that pierced every atom of the entity. The beast's scream was a soul-rending wail, darkness unraveling as holy fire consumed it from within, threads of shadow dissolving into nothingness.

With one final, transcendent surge of divine fury, Nathan hurled the remnants downward.

They plummeted as twin comets ablaze, streaking across the sky in a blaze of glory and judgment. The impact reverberated through the valley like the hammer of God, shattering the earth. Flanking peaks crumbled in apocalyptic fury, avalanches of stone thundering down to entomb the entity's ashen remains beneath an eternal grave of rubble.

A profound silence descended, heavy with the afterglow of a heavenly miracle.

The valley exhaled, the shadow's oppression lifting like a veil torn asunder.

Gabriel's heart thundered in his chest as he launched skyward, wings unfurling in a blaze of urgent light, carrying him toward the smoldering scar in the valley where the mountains had kissed the sky in ruin. Every beat of those mighty wings screamed hope—Nathan is alive. He has to be. The air still crackled with residual divinity, the scent of ozone and scorched stone thick in his throat, but beneath it all lingered the bitter tang of fear.

He landed hard amid the devastation, boots crunching into shattered rock, dust swirling like ghosts around him. His eyes— sharp, ancient, accustomed to both glory and grief—scanned the chaos: toppled peaks reduced to jagged teeth, boulders the size of houses strewn like discarded toys, a crater still glowing faintly at its heart. But no Nathan. No familiar silhouette rising from the wreckage. Only silence, heavy and accusing. Smoke still swirled miles into the air from all the devastation making it very difficult to discern if any mountain was still intact for quite some time.

Tyler and Souta stumbled after some time after him, small legs pumping desperately through the debris. Their faces were streaked with dirt and tears, eyes wide with the raw terror only children can carry unfiltered. "Haba! Haba!" they cried, voices cracking on the name that had become their anchor, their hero, their father in all but blood. Tiny hands clawed at immovable slabs of stone, fingernails scraping uselessly, sobs wrenching from their chests in waves of pure, shattering agony. They wanted to see him—anything of him—a hand, a smile, a sign that the man who had carried them through darkness was not gone forever.

Gabriel dropped to his knees beside them, wings folding protectively as he gathered the boys into his arms. Their small bodies shook against him, grief pouring out in hot, endless tears. He held them tightly, his own throat closing around unshed sorrow, whispering broken comforts in a voice that trembled for the first time in centuries. "He's here... somewhere... hold on..."

Then he rose, determination hardening into something unbreakable. Power surged through his veins—celestial strength long restrained—and he thrust his hands toward the nearest boulder, massive as a temple cornerstone. Golden light flared along his arms as he lifted, muscles straining under the weight of mountain and miracle. One by one, he heaved aside the fallen giants, each grunt of effort a prayer, each stone rolled away a plea. Sweat beaded on his brow, mingling with dust, but still— nothing. Nobody. No breath. Only deeper layers of ruin.

The boys clung to his legs, weeping louder now, their hope fraying thread by thread.

And then—the earth answered.

A low, subterranean rumble rolled through the valley, subtle at first, like the groan of awakening stone. The ground shivered beneath their feet. Dust sifted downward. Then a sharper tremor, violent, sudden—a pulse from below.

A small explosion erupted at the crater's center—not destructive, but radiant. Rock shards burst outward in a halo of light, and from the heart of the collapse, a single hand thrust upward through the rubble.

Nathan's hand.

Fingers splayed, strong and mighty with effort, skin shining in white glow and golden symbols etched by God Himself. Not merely lit from within, but radiating—pure, white-gold luminescence pouring from every pore, veins traced in holy fire. The light swelled outward in pulsing waves, cracking the remaining stones apart like eggshells, illuminating the night with a dawn that refused to wait for morning.

The boys froze, tears suspended on their cheeks, mouths open in silent wonder. Gabriel's wings flared wide, eyes blazing with awe and relief so profound it bordered on pain. The light intensified, pushing back the darkness that had dared to claim victory, until the entire wreckage was bathed in glory.

Slowly, majestically, more of the rubble shifted and fell away. Nathan emerged—not broken, not defeated, but transformed— his body aglow, along with the armor of God glowing radiantly with resurrection power, eyes burning with the same fire that had consumed the enemy. He lowered his blade slowly, exhaling a breath that carried the exhaustion of a warrior, the peace of a victor, and the quiet gratitude of a man who had sufficiently been used in God's battle against evil.

Alive.

Victorious. A soul forever changed. And the valley itself seemed to breathe again, as if creation itself exhaled in wonder at the

man who had walked through death and returned with dawn in
his hands.

(30) The Chariot Descends and Life Marches On

Nathan emerged from the fury of battle untouched, his garments without singe, his body without wound, his spirit radiant and whole. Just as the Lord had protected Shadrach, Meshach, and Abednego in the heart of the blazing fiery furnace—walking with them unharmed, their bonds loosened, their faces shining brighter than before—so had God shielded Nathan. Divine fire had raged around him, yet it only polished his faith, leaving him with an otherworldly glow that made the people gasp in awe. The air itself seemed to shimmer with the glory that rested upon him.

The camp erupted in jubilation. Men, women, and children danced before the Lord with timbrels and shouts of praise, their voices rising like incense. The victory was not merely won by sword or strategy, but by the hand of the Almighty who fights for His own.

Then, a crackle of radio static broke through to Gabriel. The voice from the northern contingent burst with astonishment: "A force of pure white light descended—brighter than the sun at noon! The earth trembled, fire roared through the blocked pass, and the mountain itself crumbled in another place, carving a new roadway wide and clear. All paths are open now! The northern tribes that were prevented from moving are now freely enroute toward the gathering!"

Gabriel's heart swelled. The Lord had moved mountains—literally—for His people.

Mere moments later, Nathan stood wrapped in the arms of his husband and their children, with laughter and tears mingling as they clung to one another. The family was whole, the battle behind them, the future bright.

Then the sky answered.

A chariot of fire descended from the heavens—horses of flame pulling a vehicle of blazing glory, the roar of its arrival like a thousand winds. The people fell silent, falling to their knees. This was no ordinary sight; it echoed the ancient day when Elijah, the great prophet, was taken up without tasting death, carried away in a whirlwind and fire to be with the Lord.

An unseen voice spoke to Nathan, gentle yet commanding: "Come up hither."

Nathan turned to Gabriel, his eyes filled with a sorrow deeper than any battlefield could hold. With trembling hands, he slipped off his wedding rings—the simple bands that had sealed their vows through every trial—and pressed them into Gabriel's palm. He closed Gabriel's fingers around them, holding the hand tight.

"Don't look at them until I've gone," Nathan whispered, voice breaking. "Know this: I did not mean for this to happen. I never intended to leave for heaven before you. I planned to grow old with you, to chase many more adventures side by side. But the Lord has called me now. Just... be sure you have those adventures with our boys." He smiled through tears, glancing at their children. "That's right—*our* boys."

Gabriel could only nod, throat too tight for words.

The heavenly escort urged Nathan forward. He stepped toward the chariot, pausing once to blow kisses—soft, radiant, heavenly—toward his family, toward the people who had fought beside him, toward the life he had loved so fiercely.

Then, in a blinding flash brighter than lightning, the chariot of fire lifted. With a rush like thunder receding, it vanished into the heavens.

The ground was still. The air carried the faint scent of holy fire.

Nathan was gone—taken without death, escorted into glory, just as the faithful few before him.

The people stood in hushed wonder, hearts torn between the sharp edge of grief and the radiant swell of awe. At last, Gabriel opened his hand, gazing down at the rings Nathan had pressed into his palm. They were no longer the simple bands he himself had forged long ago, etched with the bold Batman symbol that once spoke of Nathan's playful strength and quiet heroism. In their place, something wondrous had occurred—a divine alchemy that mirrored the changed lives Nathan had touched.

The original designs had melted away, reformed by an unseen hand into two strong, intertwined hearts that encircled a single, glowing ruby at the center. The gem burned with an inner fire, deep crimson like the chariot that had carried Nathan home, symbolizing the unbreakable union of love, faith, and sacrifice. The rings felt warm still, as if Nathan's very touch lingered, a quiet promise that what God joins endures beyond the veil.

The journey ahead would be long, the road southward winding through valleys once barred and mountains once crumbled. Yet the promise held firm: God protects, God provides, and one day, all would stand reunited in the presence of the One who calls His own home.

With hearts heavy yet lifted, the tribes turned toward that gathering place—packing tents, gathering provisions, mending harnesses—as they moved onward, carrying both sorrow and unshakable hope. For the Lord had shown Himself mighty once more, transforming not only paths and mountains, but the very tokens of love left behind.

In the days and weeks that followed, the miracle of reunion unfolded like a long-awaited dawn. The remaining tribes trickled in from every corner of the earth—encampments in the frozen north, barricaded by walls of ice and snow that had suddenly melted and parted; deep valleys now open and welcoming; parched deserts where hidden springs bubbled anew; tangled jungles where paths cleared as if by invisible hands; and from oceans wide, where ships found safe harbor at last.

They came, and they came, until the gathering place swelled with the fullness of promise. The final count stood at exactly 12,144—a number that echoed the sealed servants of God in ancient prophecy, yet now alive, breathing, and whole. The largest contingents arrived from the rugged north, the heart of the central lands, and the vibrant expanses of South America, their faces etched with the same awe and gratitude that had marked Nathan's own journey.

Every soul found a place to live—tents gave way to sturdy homes, and as the people grew in number and spirit, more dwellings rose. The land itself seemed to expand in welcome.

Songs filled the air once more: ancient melodies of ancestral reunion, vibrant hymns of the living, and triumphant choruses proclaiming the prophecy revealed and accomplished. Festivals, long dormant, were revitalized with dancing, feasting, and fires that burned late into the night.

Near the gathering estate of Gabriel and his sons, a monument was raised—a towering statue in the likeness of Nathan, captured in the moment of his ascent. He stood heroic and serene, eyes lifted heavenward, one hand extended as if still blowing those final kisses. Flames of carved stone licked at his feet, evoking the chariot of fire that had carried him home. The people called it the Monument of the Foreign Fire: a tribute to the man God had used mightily, a stranger who became brother, protector, and faithful witness.

A special song was composed in his honor, its verses carried on the wind whenever the people gathered:

"Foreign Fire, called from afar, shielded in blaze, yet never scarred. Rings of love he gave away, to walk the path the Lord ordained that day. Nathan, faithful, taken high, in chariot of flame, you touch the sky."

Amid the swelling joy of reunion, quieter moments of remembrance bloomed like night flowers in the gathering dusk. One evening, as the sun dipped low behind the southern hills, painting the sky in hues of amber and rose, Gabriel sat with his sons, Tyler and Souta, on the wide porch of their home. Below them, the bustling gathering place hummed with life—distant laughter, the crackle of festival fires—but here, on the porch, time seemed to pause. The air hung thick with the comforting scent of woodsmoke and the sweet, heady perfume of blooming night flowers.

Gabriel opened his hand slowly again, revealing the wedding rings Nathan had entrusted to him. The metal still carried a faint, lingering warmth. He gazed at the two strong hearts now intertwined seamlessly, encircling the radiant ruby at the center, and sighed a long, deep breath. It glowed, reminding him of the living embodiment of love found in his Nathan, who was refined through trial and unbreakable in his mind, even in his absence.

"He always said we'd grow old together," Gabriel murmured, voice low and steady, though his eyes betrayed the ache. "Adventures on every horizon, side by side. But the Lord had another plan—one we cannot understand, one that called him higher."

Tyler leaned forward, his own eyes glistening in the fading light. "He was so strong, Dad. He was never seemingly afraid. He told me once that if the fire came for him, he'd walk right into it smiling—because he knew who walked beside him."

Souta, the youngest, reached out and traced the edge of the intertwined hearts with a careful finger, as if afraid to disturb the miracle. "He called us 'our boys,'" he whispered. "Like we were all his, from the very start. I miss his laugh—the way it made everything feel... possible."

The three sat in companionable silence then, letting the memories wash over them like a gentle tide: battles fought shoulder to shoulder, quiet nights of shared prayer under starlit skies, the steady way Nathan's presence had turned every hardship into something bearable, even holy.

The celebration swelled that night into a mass gathering. Gabriel and Nathan's other family had been briefed on what had happened and were chartered directly to the estate by Gabriel's plane. They had arrived not more than 30 minutes prior to the start of the celebration. Hallie arrived, radiant and strong, accompanied by Bill Goldberg—whose booming presence brought smiles—and Tyler's mom, who carried stories of Nathan from the earlier days. They were ushered into the heart of the festivities, where drums and voices rose in unison.

There, amid the throng, Gabriel and the boys shared Nathan's story once more: how he had aspired to be a light in darkness, a husband who loved fiercely, a father who chose them daily. They spoke of his final moments—the chariot of fire, the rings pressed into Gabriel's hand, the heavenly kisses blown to all who watched.

Hallie's Perspective: Echoes of Fire and Reunion

I stepped into the gathering place under a sky that felt too vast, too alive with stars that seemed to whisper secrets of the divine. The air hummed with drums and voices—songs I'd never heard, but that stirred something ancient in my soul, like echoes from a forgotten dream. Bill Goldberg walked beside me, his massive frame a comforting shadow, and Tyler's mom clutched my arm, her eyes wide with the same mix of wonder and trepidation I felt. We'd been summoned here, pulled from our ordinary lives into this whirlwind of prophecy and miracle, and now we stood amid a sea of reunited tribes, their faces glowing in the firelight.

They told us about Nathan. Gabriel's voice was steady, but his eyes... oh, they carried the weight of loss and glory intertwined. He spoke of Nathan's aspirations—to be a beacon of faith, a husband who loved without reservation, a father who bridged worlds with his unyielding heart. And then the story of his departure: not in death's cold grasp, but in a chariot of blazing fire, ascending like Elijah of old. Taken without pain, without farewell's full sting, but leaving behind rings and promises and a void that echoed in every laugh around us.

I couldn't help but replay it in my mind as the festival swirled. Nathan, the "Foreign Fire," they called him—a stranger who had woven himself into this tapestry of tribes. I'd known him differently, back when life was simpler, before battles and heavenly summons. He was the one who'd always seen potential in the broken, who'd joked through storms and prayed with a fire that warmed everyone near. Hearing how God had protected him, unscathed in battle like those Hebrew boys in the furnace, made my chest tighten. Why him? Why now? But then, looking at Gabriel and the boys—Tyler with his quiet strength, Souta with that spark of mischief—I understood. Nathan hadn't left them empty; he'd left them ignited.

As the monument loomed nearby, its stone flames flickering in the torchlight, I felt a pull. The statue captured him perfectly: resolute, radiant, hand outstretched. I touched its base, whispering a prayer of my own. "You did well, Nathan. You showed us all how to burn bright without burning out."

The songs rose again, pulling me into the dance. Bill clapped along, his grin breaking through the solemnity, and Tyler's mom wiped tears that were equal parts joy and sorrow. Here, among the 12,144, I wasn't just an outsider anymore. I was part of the story—a witness to how faith reshapes worlds, crumbles mountains, and calls the faithful home.

In the quiet moments, as Gabriel shared more reminiscences, I saw my own life reflected: the valleys I'd crossed, the barriers that had melted away. Nathan's legacy wasn't just in the monument or the songs; it was in us, urging us to live with that same fierce love. And as the night deepened, I knew—I'd carry his fire forward, too.

Hallie's heart felt heavier than the southern stars overhead as she wandered the edges of the gathering place that evening. The monument to Nathan stood sentinel nearby, its stone form bathed in the soft glow of torchlight, and she found herself drawn back to it again and again. Losing her second-best friend in so few years—the first taken by a madman years ago, now Nathan swept up in divine fire—left a quiet ache that no festival drum could fully drown out. She stood reverent before the statue, fingers brushing the carved flames at its base, whispering a prayer that felt both raw and sacred.

Why him, Lord? And why now, when everything else is finally coming together? The questions swirled, but beneath them lay something new: a pull toward this place, these people, this renewed family of tribes. The 12,144 souls around her moved with purpose and joy, their songs weaving threads of hope she hadn't known she needed.

She'd noticed the glances, too subtle at first, then warmer. Handsome men from the northern contingents, strong and steady-eyed, from the central heartlands, and even a few from the vibrant southern groups. They carried themselves with the same quiet faith Nathan had embodied, and more than once, a smile lingered longer than courtesy demanded. It stirred something in her— not distraction, but possibility. A life here might mean more than mourning; it might mean belonging.

Tyler's mom had already begun to weave herself into the fabric of the tribe, laughing easily with a kind-eyed elder from the central lands, their shoulders brushing as they shared stories by the fire. If she could find a place so naturally, why not Hallie?

The thought crystallized as the night deepened. She could stay. She *wanted* to stay.

The next morning, with resolve steadying her steps, Hallie approached Gabriel at the estate. He was on the porch again, the same one where he'd shared memories with his sons, the air still scented with woodsmoke and night-blooming flowers. She waited until the boys had wandered off to help with the morning preparations before speaking.

"Gabriel," she began, voice soft but firm, "I've been thinking... about Nathan, about this place, about what comes next. Losing him—it's hit me hard. Harder than I expected. But being here, seeing how the tribes have come together, how faith has moved mountains... it feels like home in a way I haven't felt in years."

She met his eyes, steady despite the tremor in her chest. "I've seen the work that needs doing—the gardens to tend, the stories to preserve, the children to teach, the festivals to prepare. If there's any way I could contribute, earn my place here... I'd like to ask. Not as a guest passing through, but as someone who wants to stay. To be part of the family of the tribe."

Gabriel regarded her for a long moment, the weight of Nathan's absence softening into something gentler in his gaze. A small, knowing smile touched his lips.

"Nathan always said the Lord brings people exactly where they're meant to be," he replied quietly. "And He doesn't waste a heart like yours. There's always room here—for hands that serve, for voices that sing, for souls that seek. We'll find the right place for you, Hallie. Welcome home."

The gathering place welcomed her not as an outsider, but as one more thread in the tapestry God was weaving. Hallie felt the ache of loss ease, just a little, replaced by the gentle promise of new beginnings—rooted in faith, friendship, and the enduring fire that Nathan had helped kindle in them all.

The tribes were whole again. The prophecy stood fulfilled. Nathan's legacy burned bright—not in absence, but in the lives he had touched, the faith he had kindled, and the promise that one day, beyond the veil, every tear would be wiped away.

The songs continued onward, taught to new generations, and the people walked forward together, reunited, redeemed, and forever marked by the Foreign Fire who had shown them the way home.